Flight Plan

An Aviation Romance

Lynn Campbell

Veronica Freeland

For my father Dana Nuckols,

whose presence returned to my life in early adulthood. I am deeply grateful for the time we shared.

For Jeff Fahrlander,

a true friend to David, taken from us too soon. Your spirit endures in our memories.

And to the aviation community at Deer Valley Airport,

a family in its own right. I am honored to have you as part of my family's journey.

Contents

Prologue

Daniel Gerrard stood with his daughter outside the door of the four-person suite at The Village at Alpine Valley. Mackenzie was all moved in. He pulled her close. *This is it.*

When he felt her gently pull away, Daniel let go and held her at arm's length. Tears stung the back of his eyelids. *Not here, not now.*

She looked up into his face. Her liquid-brown eyes held all the excitement of the upcoming adventure.

He brushed some honey-colored hair off her brow. "Okay. If you need anything or get homesick, call me, your mom, Grandma and Grandpa G, or Nini and Papa."

"I will, Dad. Don't worry. I'm going to be fine here."

"Okay then."

He pulled her close again, this time only for a moment. After a quick peck on her cheek, he turned and walked purposefully past the pictures and identical brown doors toward the elevator. Within moments, his Dodge Ram turned toward the setting sun across Interstate 25 to the hotel where he and Mackenzie had stayed the previous night.

Once in his room, he looked around. All of her luggage was gone. Her toiletry bag was no longer on the counter by the sink. Two perfectly made queen beds took up the center of the room. Only one bed would be occupied tonight. Tomorrow, he would continue on from

Colorado Springs to Phoenix, Arizona for a new career and a life that was now truly his own.

He sat heavily on the bed and dropped his forehead into his hand.

Aubrey Cassen circled the brush and cactus-studded area of the stranded off-road vehicle twice, indicating to the men and boy on the ground that they were seen, and help would arrive soon. Her search and rescue partner talked to the Civil Air Patrol on the Cessna 182's radio, reporting the exact location of the missing Razor riders. Julio beamed at her. She then turned and flashed a smile at the two teen CAP cadets in the back seat. One gave her a thumbs up.

The plane hit a bump in the hot-air turbulence. "We're getting low on fuel. Help is on the way. We're heading back." She rocked her wings at the stranded motorists and banked the red, white, and blue plane south toward Deer Valley Airport.

After landing on runway 25 Left, Aubrey radioed Skyways Aviation to send the refueling truck.

When Aubrey and her three passengers exited the airplane, the Emergency Services Officer went out to meet them.

"The disabled Razor has been loaded onto a tow truck, and the three off roaders will be taken to a local hospital to be checked out."

The two cadets nudged each other and let out whoops.

"Good eyes, you two. Thanks for your help." She shook hands with both.

One young man glanced at the ground then shyly at her eyes.

"Okay guys, call your parents and go get a snack," Julio said, motioning toward the small white and brick building.

"Race you," the shy one said to the other.

Then, despite the August temperatures, both boys ran toward CAP headquarters.

Once the plane was tied down and refueled, Aubrey headed to her shiny blue Dodge Challenger. A white piece of paper fluttered under her driver's side windshield wiper. As soon as she unfolded the paper, she saw the Cassen and Harper Enterprises letterhead and her father's large, flowing cursive. Her heartbeat quickened.

Aubrey,

We need to talk. Please call.

Dad

With a sigh, she tore the paper into pieces.

Chapter One

Daniel peered out from under the wing of the Piper Cherokee when he heard an unfamiliar female voice. A woman with long, pale blonde hair had entered the hangar of Skyways Aviation, the Fixed Based Operation where he had started work two weeks ago. The FBO's owner, Nate, walked over to her, and they briefly embraced. Nate's six-foot two height dwarfed her five-foot five frame.

Daniel was the first back from lunch, so bits of conversation floated his way in the now quiet hangar. Something about a recent trip to San Diego and the upcoming annual inspection on her airplane.

"Come on over here. I'll introduce you to the new guy." Nate was leading her towards him.

"Hey Dan, come on out for a second."

Daniel slid out from under the wing, halfway through a brake job.

"Aubrey, this is Dan, our new Airframe and Powerplant mechanic from Montana."

Daniel quickly wiped his hands on a shop cloth.

She took his hand in a confident and professional manner. "Well, on behalf of the Deer Valley Airport Pilot's Association, welcome."

She was in her late 20s or early 30s, stunning blue eyes and a heart-shaped face. He took a cursory glance at her left hand which was bare of any jewelry.

"I've heard so many great things about flying into Montana. I understand there are a lot of small airports and grass strips."

"There are. You should fly up there sometime."

"It's on my Bucket List." Aubrey's smile lit up her whole face.

In a moment, her attention was turned back to Nate. "Let me show you what I'm talking about with the fuel selector valve."

She and Nate turned and walked toward a red, white, and blue V-Tail Bonanza, giving him a glimpse of her graceful legs leading up to some nice-fitting shorts.

He eased himself back under the Piper's wing. *Not now, not yet. She's probably taken anyway.*

Aubrey started up her plane after Nate made a slight adjustment to her fuel selector valve. She then hit the talk button for the radio. "Deer Valley Ground, Bonanza 6282 Romeo requesting permission to cross the runways to north hangars."

"82 Romeo cross Runway 2-5, then hold short at runway 7."

"Cross 2-5, hold short at 7. 82 Romeo."

Using the rudder pedals, she steered the plane from the tarmac in front of Skyways to the taxiway.

The new A and P was not what she expected. Months ago, when Geoff announced that he would retire at the end of July, Nate attended both local and out-of-state job fairs to hire a replacement.

"82 Romeo, cross Runway 7."

The sky to the north and east was clouding up. The local news predicted another monsoon dust storm tonight. Damn. It would probably hit about the time she was driving north to fill-in at the newborn nursery.

Nate said he hired someone from a trade school in Montana who would start at the end of August. She had expected a kid right out of high school or college. Instead, the new A and P was a little older than she was, probably mid-30s and single, judging from his left hand. The first thing she noticed when he climbed out from under the wing was a gorgeous combination of amber eyes set off by honey colored hair.

Daniel pulled a Piper Comanche out of the Skyways hangar using the Best Tugs apparatus. Now three weeks on the job, things were starting to flow. He turned toward the terminal when he caught a glimpse of sunlight on blonde hair. Aubrey was leaning on an Asian guy. The two were laughing as they walked from her parked plane toward the building.

He turned away, disconnecting the tug, but then turned right back. Aubrey and her companion embraced before he went into the terminal, and she turned back toward her plane. Daniel walked purposefully to the hangar before she could notice him looking.

Yep. A woman like her had to be taken. It was just as well.

Aubrey sat on the carpeted floor of Nate and Justine's guest house taking apart a metal shelving unit.

Justine came in and started taking apart another unit. "Well, that's the last of the tax boxes. Thank you for coming in on a day off to help."

Aubrey shrugged. "No problem. It's the least I can do since you rented it to me when I needed it. So, who's coming?"

"A woman and her daughter. Refugees from Ukraine."

"Nice."

"Yes. Speaking of nice, our new A and P is not only a nice guy, but he's also easy on the eyes. Around your age too."

Aubrey looked toward the ceiling and sighed.

"I'm just saying."

"Yeah. You're just saying. How's he working out?"

"Great. He does excellent work. We want to keep him, that's for sure."

Nate entered the small living room and started packing up the shelving parts Aubrey had taken apart. "Yeah, all he needs is some Zonie gal with a lot to offer. Then he'll stay for sure."

"You too, huh?"

"Sorry...but not really."

Justine looked up at Nate, the warmth in their gazes melting Aubrey's heart.

Over the next few weeks, Daniel noticed that Aubrey seemed to pop in often at Skyways. Sometimes for a reason, other times to say hi and hang out. She would ask Ricardo, another A and P, about his wife's pregnancy. Once, Daniel walked into the break room to find Aubrey and Sasha on the couch at the back of the room. Aubrey was holding Sasha's hand. A quick assessment told him the 20 something A and P was crying over a breakup with her boyfriend. Aubrey seemed to belong everywhere in the small FBO.

One evening at the end of his shift, he noticed a dark green gift bag on the break room's table with his name on it. Inside it was a burgundy, reusable water bottle along with packets of Liquid IV, Emergen C, Salud, and Ultima drink-mix packets. The note read:

Daniel,

Welcome to Arizona and Skyways. I know you're not used to the Arizona heat. Here are some electrolyte mixes to try. Dehydration can be a real bitch.

Aubrey

When he exited the building through the lobby door, he shielded his eyes from a gust of gritty wind that blew under the blue and white awning. The sky below the clouds was muted and dirty.

Yes, it was hot, but he had worked outdoors most of his working life. He knew how to stay hydrated. Like Arizona's dry heat, humid summers in Montana also posed a dehydration risk. Still, it was nice of her to think of him.

Aubrey stopped off at Skyways to pay her monthly fuel bill. Justine was not at the front desk. Aubrey took a moment to observe the hangar through the huge window behind Justine's desk. The place was a buzz of activity on this Wednesday morning. The new guy Daniel leaned over the engine of a Cessna 210 intently talking to Sasha. He had an angular face and stern jawline. This time, his hair was mostly covered in a Skyways ballcap, but some peaked out the brim and the back.

Now Sasha was talking to Daniel. She pushed her long, light brown braid from her shoulder to her back then pointed at something on the plane's engine. He nodded, then turned his attention toward the Cessna's engine while she walked toward another plane. Daniel moved to where his back was to the window. He filled out his jeans and Skyways T-shirt nicely.

Where is Justine anyway?

Aubrey opened the lobby's back door and entered the hangar. When she walked past the Cessna 210, Daniel was engrossed in his work. Ricardo's shoes were visible through the open baggage compartment of a Beech Baron indicating he was working inside the tail. Small and thin, he often worked in the tight spaces. Toward the back of the hangar, Nate and Ray, the retired Air Force A and P, were lowering an engine to the floor. Once the engine was safely on the ground, she called out to Nate.

"Hey Aubrey." He put his ball cap over his graying blonde hair that reached just above his shoulders.

"Hey, I need to pay my bill, but Justine's not at her desk."

"Yeah, she had an appointment this morning. I'll take care of you."

As they walked by the 210, a cell phone rang chirping crickets. Daniel straightened up from leaning over the engine and took a phone out of his pocket.

"Hey Mac! . . .Good to hear."

Daniel's half of the conversation faded as he walked out of the hangar.

He was clearly happy to hear from whomever called, but her skin prickled. The hairs on her arms were still standing even when she reached her car. The tone. Her father sounded like that after every flawless report card she brought home and with every award she earned.

Stomach growling, Daniel walked into the break room to find Justine having a late lunch. Her warm brown eyes, much like Mackenzie's, lit up at his sight. Her short, light auburn hair reminded him of his mother. Of course, he wasn't going to tell her that.

He wetted a paper towel and wiped it over his face. "I didn't know a tailwheel could be so stubborn. Worse than my daughter when she sets her mind to something."

"That's right. You're a single dad."

"Not exactly. My ex and I raised her together."

"How long you been divorced?"

"Fifteen years."

"That long? I'm surprised some gal didn't snap you up before now."

He chuckled and shrugged. "I guess relationships aren't my strong suit. For one reason or another, they didn't last."

"Well don't you dare give up. I was twenty-nine, divorced, and living back on my parents' ranch in New Mexico. Then this tall, strapping man came into the airport diner I was working at." She motioned in the direction of Nate's office. "I had sworn off men and made it clear that other than serving him, I would have nothing to do with him. But he kept finding reasons to fly in and eat at the diner."

"Wouldn't they call that harassment nowadays?"

She shrugged. "Not the way he went about it. He kept showing me who he was. His gentle persistence and kindness won me over. The rest, as they say, is history."

Her eyes were moist when she squeezed his hand. "There's someone out there for you. Don't you lose heart."

Chapter Two

Daniel entered the hangar from the lobby right as Aubrey parked her Bonanza and climbed out onto the wing. White denim shorts hugged her hips and shapely buttocks. *Perfect timing.*

Daniel approached her with a smile while she took a large paper bag out of the baggage compartment. A hot breeze fluttered her teal green top carrying a light scent of citrus and rose his way.

"I see we're starting the annual for your plane. I'll back it into the hangar in a moment."

"Great. I brought bagels for the break room." Aubrey headed for the back of the hangar, greeting his coworkers along the way.

He attached the tug to the nosewheel when a wrench clattered to the ground.

"Shit!"

Ricardo clutched his arm. Blood seeped through his fingers. Daniel raced toward him mentally reviewing his first-aid training.

"Somebody get Aubrey!" Sasha shouted.

Aubrey barged through the door from the break room. She pulled some latex gloves from her purse and ran to Ricardo before Daniel could get to him.

"My wrench slipped! My arm went right into the sheet metal!

She'll need the first aid kit. Daniel turned toward the shelf near the sink, but Ray had already taken the kit down and brought it to Aubrey.

She examined Ricardo's injured arm. "That looks deep enough for stitches."

Aubrey pulled out some absorbent cotton pads and gauze tape which she wrapped tightly around his wiry forearm. "That will hold it until I can get you to the ER.

By now, Justine was in the hangar handing Aubrey her keys. "Take the suburban."

Daniel watched as Aubrey ushered Ricardo out.

After her annual inspection was complete, Aubrey seemed to have constant fill-in-nurse calls. Now with a free Thursday, she spent the afternoon practicing engine-out landings at Willliams Field. After landing back at Deer Valley, Aubrey taxied to Skyways where Daniel met her at her plane.

"Need a refuel." She climbed down the wing and headed for the restroom.

When she returned, Daniel was replacing the left fuel cap and heading for the right wing. Crickets chirped on his phone.

"Hey there." His eyes seemed to light up. "Uh oh. I'm in trouble now aren't I...Okay. As soon as I'm done with what I'm doing, I'll send it via Zelle...Sorry. Love you."

Daniel looked sheepish when he ended the call. "Forgot my daughter Mackenzie's allowance. Her mother and I switch off months sending money to her account."

"Where is she?"

"University of Colorado in Colorado Springs." He put the fuel cap back on the right wing.

While she climbed back into her plane, Daniel walked toward the hangar with his phone out likely doing the Zelle transaction. A breeze ruffled his hair. A child in college? He was either older than he looked or he started young.

Daniel was just finishing lunch when Ray walked in through the gray metal door, his salt and pepper hair disheveled from being under the dash of a Cessna.

"I know you're just having lunch, but what are you doing for dinner tonight?" He ran a hand through his hair.

"I was thinking of having a frozen pizza at home. Do you have a better idea?"

"Yeah. We're all going to The Q Bar and Grill. They have an amazing fish fry on Friday nights."

"Fish in the desert. I don't know. Don't get me wrong, I love living here but..."

"It's pollock or cod flown in fresh from Alaska." Ray retrieved his lunch from the fridge.

Daniel got up to retrieve another soda. "In that case, I'm in."

Daniel found a place to park and entered the slump block bar. It didn't look like much on the outside, but it reminded him of home once he walked in. Taxidermized animals of all kinds decorated the walls among the televisions broadcasting various sports. Most of them featured the baseball playoffs in preparation for the World Series. Bar and grill establishments like this were all over Montana along the highways and in small towns.

The place was packed. His coworkers sat at a long, curved booth between the entrance and the jukebox. A red Budweiser sign glowed above the booth. Across from their booth were some occupied four-person booths. On the other side of a barrier wall, were more four-person booths, also occupied, and beyond them, two pool tables. He took another sweep of the room. Nothing seemed amiss.

He sat next to Nate and ordered a Pilsner on draft from the tank-top clad server.

"Aubrey will be joining us when she gets off work," Nate said offhandedly. "She said go ahead and order."

Daniel nodded. "Ray said the fish fry was excellent."

"Order it. You won't be disappointed."

Partway through fish, fries, and coleslaw that lived up to the hype, Aubrey arrived and sat next to Daniel. Her navy-blue scrubs neither hid nor accentuated her figure. Her hair in a tight French braid reached the top of her shoulders.

"Hey. Glad you could make it." She nudged his shoulder.

The hours flew by, and when Nate and Justine left, he turned. Only he and Aubrey remained at the large booth. *Start another conversation or offer to walk her to her car?*

Aubrey took a last swig of her beer. "I've been wondering. You seem awfully young to have a child in college. Not trying to be nosy, but how old were you when she was born?"

"It's fine. I was seventeen, a senior in high school. She knows she wasn't planned, but her mother, Jen, and I made sure she knew she wasn't a mistake."

Her eyes softened. "Well, she's clearly lucky to have you as a father."

Daniel looked down for a moment. "It's getting late. Come on. I'll walk you to your car."

A commotion at the long wooden bar caught Daniel's attention. A man who'd clearly had too much to drink was becoming belligerent.

"Stay here," he said to Aubrey, then walked slowly over to the man, focusing on being calm and relaxed. "Hey man. How are you doing?"

"Who the hell are you?"

"Just another customer." The smell of liquor made him recoil but he quickly brought it under control.

"Well, just another customer. I've had a shitty week, and I came here to have a good time, but this asshole won't pour me another Jim Beam!"

"You've had a hell of a week and you're ready for some fun. Come on over here. We'll figure out what to do."

The man stumbled as he got off the barstool. Daniel caught him, and they walked to an empty, high-top table between the entrance and the patio.

Daniel stood to the side of the man. "So, what can you do to have more of a good time tonight? You hungry? Do you have a favorite streaming series? You know you're not safe to drive."

The man sighed and relaxed. "No, I'm not."

Daniel called an Uber while the bartender brought the man a meal on the house. A few minutes later, Daniel walked him out and watched the Uber drive off.

He returned to Aubrey. "Sorry about that."

Aubrey collected her purse. "No problem. The bartender clearly had his hands full."

Their hands brushed when they both reached for the door.

"You sure seemed to know what to do."

"I've dealt with a lot of intoxicated people...A lot."

"Yeah? Doing what?"

"Montana Highway Patrol."

Aubrey's eyebrows shot up in curious surprise, but the sparkle in her eyes was all Daniel needed to know his answer impressed her.

Chapter Three

The following Monday morning, Daniel put his lunch in the fridge then unloaded his wallet, keys and holstered pistol into his locker. He was securing the lock when Nate and Ray walked in. Ray started the coffee maker while Nate unloaded a bag of napkins and plasticware into the cabinets and drawers. He then turned toward Daniel with a smile.

"Dan, what is your after-work schedule like this week?"

"I'm open. Why?"

"It's my tradition to take my new employees out for beers and appetizers after they have had time to settle in. Tomorrow after work?"

"Sure."

Ray turned from the coffee maker. "You're going to love TAV. The wings are great."

Daniel smiled. "I'm looking forward to it."

The door swung open, and Sasha and Ricardo entered bantering back and forth as usual. With a lightness in his heart, Daniel headed for the hangar to finish up last nights' repair.

Aubrey used her volunteer card to walk into the employee entrance of the Arizona Humane Society through the spacious, nearly empty break room. She made her way to the recovery ward. Vets and vet techs scurried around metal exam tables and rows of kennels checking and tending to various dogs and cats. *Sam should be here.* She finally spotted him at a table bandaging up an unconscious cat.

"Hi there, Aubrey. What brings you in today?"

He turned toward her, and his ice-blue eyes glinted. Warmth radiated from her core as he took in the sight of her in her Foo Fighters t-shirt and her favorite jeans. Five years ago, they had flown to San Diego together to see the show followed by a night to remember in their hotel room.

"Dropping off donations from the airport's pet supply drive."

He adjusted his glasses on his nose. "Great. Let me put this little guy into a kennel and I'll help you unload."

When they reached her Challenger, he moved a strand of hair out of her face then ran his hand through her hair down to her back. "I was planning to call you soon. Would you like to come over to my place tomorrow night?"

She smiled as the warmth returned, reaching her abdomen and chest. "Yeah. I'll have to come over after seven since I work a day shift tomorrow. Should I have dinner at work, or will you be making one of your pizzas?"

He ran a hand over his shaved head. "You may want to eat at work. I'm sure I'll be hungry before then."

After they unloaded their boxes in the supply room, he walked her to her car. She reached her arms around the back of his neck, pulling him down for a quick peck.

TAV was another bar Daniel had driven by many times but had never gone in. It was across the street from the west end of the parallel runways. He notated the cars in the parking lot then walked in and through the alcove. Nate hadn't arrived yet. The front room with the pool table had windows looking out onto the airport and the bar's parking lot. The tables near the windows were occupied by guys or couples enjoying the happy hour. He crossed the concrete floor and turned into the dimly lit bar area where he took a booth in a back corner near the dart boards and juke box. Aerosmith's "Back in the Saddle" competed with the baseball playoffs and loud conversation.

He waved when Nate appeared in the entrance to the bar.

"Have you had a chance to look over the menu? The drunken fries are to die for." Nate eased himself into the booth opposite Daniel.

Within moments, a server in short shorts and a tank top made her way to their table.

"Hi Nate. No Justine tonight?" She set down cocktail napkins and a basket of condiments and full-size napkins.

"Not tonight. I'm checking in with Dan, our new A and P." He motioned toward Daniel. "Dan, this is Casey."

The young woman took their order and disappeared with a flip of her tied-back chocolate hair.

Nate waved at the bartender behind the long, mirror-backed bar, then turned to Daniel. "Well, I had a good feeling about you at your interview, and my feelings are usually right. You seem to be fitting right in with the Skyways family."

The server reappeared with a Scottsdale Blonde for Nate and Pilsner on draft for Daniel.

"Working at Skyways has been great. Everyone's been available to help when I need it, but you all let me do my job when I don't."

"The heat not bothering you too much?"

Daniel shrugged. "I don't have to shovel it."

Nate shielded his eyes for a moment when a couple entered the dark paneled room from the side door.

"Great to hear. This is between you and me, so I want you to be honest. Have there been any problems at work with anything, your coworkers, the customers, the work, the schedule? Me or Justine?"

"None. I'm happy to be at Skyways."

The server appeared again with plates of wings and drunken fries. Nate asked for a second round of beers.

"How are you adjusting to life after law enforcement?"

"Honestly, I'm glad to be out of it. Don't get me wrong, I took a lot of pride in my career. But I started feeling like I had seen too much, and it was taking a toll."

Nate nodded. "I can understand that. Judging from a few of the stories you've told, I don't think I could do it."

A group of four men at the high-top table next to them cheered at the baseball game on three of the five screens. Daniel looked toward one of the screens to check the score, then turned his attention back to Nate.

"With both planes and law enforcement, mistakes can be costly. But with planes, I have time to think and check. I'm not making split-second, life-or-death decisions."

Nate put his napkin on his plate. "Machines are way less stressful than the general public. Some pilots, however, can be a real pain in the ass."

Daniel laughed and clinked Nate's raised mug.

Aubrey's workday proved long and stressful, particularly with anxious and impatient parents. In the hospital's locker room, she showered, changed, and sprayed on Last Light, one of her favorite perfumes. *Ready to put this day behind me.*

She arrived at Sam's condo around 7:45 p.m. A thrill shot through her when he answered the door, and his eyes once again drank her in. The bachelor pad had been picked up and straightened. No mewing or whimpering to be heard.

"No taking work home with you tonight?"

"Not this time."

She had barely set down her purse on the end table when his arms encircled her waist, pressing her to him while thrusting his tongue deep into her mouth. He had changed clothes, but a mild scent of the shelter was still on his skin. His fingers trailed down her neck to the collar of her shirt, freeing the buttons then grabbing and kneading a breast while his lips took in her earlobe.

Her breathing quickened, but she pulled back from him. "We gonna' do it right here in the living room?"

He chuckled, shook his head, and led her by the hand toward his bedroom.

Daniel threw his trash bag over his shoulder and headed to the dumpster that stood behind his row of apartments in the Avilla Deer Valley complex. The other night, Nate said he was fitting in well with the Skyways family. And a family it was. He hadn't felt so much a part of anything since he hung up his badge. The crew at Skyways had quickly taken him in easing the regret of being on the outside with his former brothers and sisters in tan.

As he dumped his trash, a woman around his age was bringing her trash bag to the shared dumpster. A small, long-haired, white dog with black and brown spots trotted on a leash beside her. He had seen her around but from a distance. Tonight, up close, she was gorgeous in gray slacks and a coral sleeveless shirt that brought out her olive complexion. Dark-blonde hair held back in a coral clip tumbled down her back.

He held the dumpster's lid open for her.

"Thank you," she said, heaving her bag in.

Once the lid was closed, he turned to her. "No problem. I'm Daniel, I moved in a couple of months ago."

The little dog sniffed at Daniel's steel-toed shoes.

She smiled down at her pup. "Come on, Rufus. I'm sure you have the whole story of where he's been by now."

"He's not bothering me." He got down on one knee and petted the pup after allowing him to sniff his hand.

"I'm Rochelle. I've lived here for a little over a year. Are you settling in okay?"

"Yeah. It's very nice here."

"Good. Well, Rufus and I need to get to our walk. Nice meeting you."

"You as well."

Daniel turned toward his apartment, willing his eyes not to follow Rochelle's retreating form. *Arizona keeps getting hotter.*

Aubrey had the day off, as no calls came in that morning or the previous evening. The sky was heavy with low-hanging dark clouds. *No flying today. Damn. Maybe it will clear.* After cereal and coffee, she threw on a stained T-shirt and an old, torn pair of denim shorts and headed for her second home.

Aubrey grabbed a bottle of kerosene and some shop cloths out of her cabinet on the east wall of the hangar. The belly wouldn't need much cleaning after she scrubbed it down a month ago before her annual inspection.

She started at the tail, wiping in a circular motion. What was the deal with Sam a few nights ago? Their friends-with-benefits relationship had always been great. He never failed to satisfy, and she made sure it was the same for him. She prided herself in making sure her friends were well satisfied. So, what changed? He was always on the aggressive side as a lover, but that night, he finished first and in record time. Everything he did for her afterward seemed based on bringing her to the peak of desire quickly. What the-

"Hello?"

She wheeled out on her roller from under the belly to see Daniel standing next to the right wing.

"Hey. How long have you been standing there?" She stood up resting a hand on the fuselage.

"Not long. I'm delivering some parts for Nate and saw your hangar open. Thought I would say 'hi' before taking the parts in."

"Nice." Aubrey looked down at her grubbies and the black streaks down her arms.

Silence.

He looked down at the concrete floor. "Well, I should get those parts delivered." Daniel turned, then stopped and looked back. "Want some help?"

"Sure."

"Things are a little slow, so I'll be right back."

Since their conversation at The Q a week ago, this new A and P was coming more into focus. Former teen dad, ex law enforcement, likely went through a lot on both counts. His training enabled him to take control of the belligerent customer situation. Images of Daniel in a State Trooper uniform peppered her imagination. He must have looked damn hot.

Daniel took off his black Diamondbacks ballcap and wiped the sweat from his forehead with his shirt sleeve. The front of his shirt was soaked. He was about to set up another round with the pitching machine when his phone rang Jen's Popcorn ring tone. They hadn't talked since he called to tell her he had made it to Phoenix.

"Hey Daniel. Where are you? It sounds noisy."

"Batting cages. I'm thinking about joining one of the adult leagues here."

"Good for you. How is Arizona anyway?"

"Hot. The dust storms are awful, the sunsets are gorgeous, and the monsoons are like nothing we see in Montana."

"Well, I wanted to let you know that I can make it for Mackenzie's family weekend next month."

"Good. I'd have been there if you couldn't, but you know how it is asking for time off early in a new job." Daniel took a swig from his water bottle. "How are Wyatt and the boys?"

"They're great. Wyatt's new program for at-risk teens is expanding into other counties. And the boys, well, they're pre-teen boys with ADHD. I'll just say sometimes I'm glad my house is still standing."

Daniel chuckled. "You're a great mom, Jen. Glad to hear you can make it to family weekend." He pressed the end button.

It was too hot for another session and too early for outdoor batting practice even in the evening. He packed up his duffle bag and headed for the parking lot.

Jen, his first love. Had they done things in the right order, they might still be married today. But the stress of a Plan B life took its toll. Giving up baseball, going straight from high school graduation to work, toddler tantrums. None of it was conducive to maintaining the passion and tenderness they originally shared. Would he ever feel that again?

Chapter Four

Daniel awoke with snippets of dreams of Montana. The only sound in the bedroom was the ceiling fan. *This isn't home. This isn't home.* It taunted.

On Saturdays in Montana, he'd call family, or go hiking with friends, or hang out with Mackenzie and see what the day would bring. If he closed his eyes, he was there again. The maple leaves were morphing from green to crimson to violet while the grassy plains glowed yellow. The Great Falls Farmer's Market vendors would be selling fresh apple cider, and all kinds of items made of pumpkin and corn. The fly-fishing tournaments were beginning. An ache began to build in his heart. He loved competing in those tournaments then going out for beers and wings afterward.

But he wasn't there, was he? Sure, Arizona had farmers markets with similar wares, but without the chill in the air and the flannels and sweaters, it wasn't the same.

With a groan, he got up, did some stretches and began doing push-ups. His muscles awakened a little more each time he pressed himself up. Then widening his arms, he let out a breath each time he moved his torso side to side in archer push-ups. His arms, upper back, and chest seemed to cheer him on as blood coursed through them.

He stood chugging water from the bottle Aubrey gave him while the breeze from the ceiling fan blew across the sweat on his T-shirt, cooling him. When he'd opened his eyes this morning, Daniel came *that* close to calling Nate to give his notice, pack his bags and head north for Montana.

Using a desk chair, he went into incline push-ups, tightening his abs to support his lower back. The lactic acid started to burn. Daniel turned, braced his arms on the chair, firmly planting his heels into the carpet. Triceps tightened as he lowered his buttocks to the floor then pressed up.

No, it hadn't been enough time yet. Of course, there would be an adjustment period where he would swing back and forth between homesickness and embracing Arizona. That was to be expected after moving to a new state where the only one he knew outside of work was a former coworker on Highway Patrol. He had to give it adequate time.

Lying on the floor, he raised his arms and legs forming his body into a V position. Twenty-eight...twenty-nine...thirty. Then bracing his hands on the carpet, he lifted his buttocks and legs slightly off the floor, arms trembling mildly, abs burning.

He lay on the soft carpet, taking deep breaths before rising for more water and another round of stretches. Now fully awake and clear-headed, he washed his face and made some breakfast.

After beautiful fall came meat-locker winter. Working in an open hangar at Skyways this winter promised to be paradise compared to what he was used to.

He sat down to eggs, multi-seed toast and apple slices. Family and friends had placed bets on how long it would be before he moved back home. Three months, six months, and his best friend who had spent time in Arizona said he wouldn't make it through September.

When he finished breakfast, he sat down on the couch to make the first of two phone calls.

After taking a moment to catch her breath, Aubrey turned. Her friend Andrew was pulling on a pair of athletic shorts.

He turned to her, smiled, and leaned down to kiss her. "I'll be right back. Don't go anywhere." His dark, almond-shaped eyes had a light behind them.

Aubrey grabbed another pillow off the floor and set it on the pillow she was lying on. "I'll be right here when you get back."

She pulled on her T-shirt and panties, then lay there listening to him pad down the hallway of his condo. Cabinets and the fridge opened and closed, followed by the whirr of a microwave. She smoothed out the gray comforter and moved a couple of red decorative pillows when he returned with a tray and a plate.

"Dinner on our shift was a while ago, but I have some egg rolls and quesadillas." He set the tray on the bed between them. "And...." He motioned to the plate. "My mother sent me some of her almond cookies. I know you really like them."

"Love them," she said, picking one up and taking a bite.

Andrew donned a T-shirt of his own and slid onto the bed. Grabbing an eggroll, he brought it to Aubrey's lips. She bit off half of it, savoring the softness and pungency of the steamed vegetables and chicken. He ate the other half. Following suit with a coy smile, she picked up a triangle of quesadilla and fed it to Andrew. Melted cheese dripped from the bitten off part. Aubrey caught it licking it off her finger before taking a bite.

Once the plates were empty, Andrew set them on the floor and turned to her with another sparkle in his eyes. Her eyes held his while she removed her T-shirt, then ran her hands up the silky black hair on the back of his head, pulling him down onto her.

Daniel rang the doorbell of the tan and brown ranch style house. A simple Halloween wreath adorned the door, but no macabre decorations embellished the front of the house or the yard.

Ray opened the door and greeted him with a bright smile. "Hey Daniel! I'm so glad you came." He motioned Daniel into the house.

When he entered the comfortable home, Vanessa was setting the last of the food on the table. Her flowery dress brought out her rosy complexion. The smell of meatloaf and roasted potatoes jogged his appetite while reminding him of home.

"Thanks for the invite." He handed Ray the frozen cheesecake he brought over for dessert.

Daniel called Ray to invite him and his wife to come over Saturday afternoon to watch the last playoff game. Turns out they had church activities, but he was invited over for meatloaf on Sunday night.

He spent Saturday doing some internet research and watching the game on his own. This Sunday was his day to man the fuel truck for Skyways as the FBO had limited hours and services on Sundays. He had just enough time to start thawing the cheesecake and shower before heading to Ray's house.

Over the wonderful dinner, Daniel shared snippets of his life in Montana while learning more about Ray's former life in the military. Vanessa took secretarial jobs throughout the relocations and deployments. Their four children were now grown and living their own lives.

"I noticed Aubrey is around Skyways a lot, but she doesn't work there," Daniel said before taking a bite of cheesecake.

"Aubrey was around before I was. From what I understand, she has been hanging around the airport since she was a teen. She worked at Skyways for a while before she became a nurse."

Daniel nodded.

"Is your question random curiosity or is there more behind it?" Vanessa chimed in, smiling.

Ray rolled his eyes and chuckled. "Come on, Ness, don't put the man on the spot. I want him to come over again."

She turned toward Daniel again. "Sorry. I didn't mean to pry."

"No problem," Daniel said. "The fact that she's attractive isn't lost on me. But I'm not looking for a relationship right now."

"Okay. I can tell you that Aubrey is not the committing type although we would all like to see her settle down and be happy with someone." Ray's eyes met Daniel's. "Tread carefully with that one."

Daniel entered the break room and began heating up the leftovers Ray and Vanessa sent home with him. Sasha sat at the table reading while she nibbled a sandwich and sipped a Diet Coke. A broken-down wall and the words No Boundaries in huge yellow letters adorned the cover.

When he sat across from her, she put down her book. Her smile lit up her brown eyes.

"Don't let me disturb you. Especially if you are on a good part."

Sasha rolled her eyes. "With this book, I wouldn't worry about it."

"In that case, I need an opinion." He pulled out his phone. "I was doing some internet research on room decor. I'm wanting to set up my office as a room for my daughter when she comes to visit at some point. She's a few years younger than you are. Can you look at some rooms I screenshotted and tell me what you think?"

Sasha took his phone and swiped through the five screenshots.

"I noticed all of the shots are heavy on green. Is green her favorite color?"

"Yeah."

"Is she a girly-girl?"

"Not even close."

"Then I don't recommend the third room. Too frilly."

"Okay. Go ahead and delete that one."

Her index finger moved twice on his phone. "Done. Is she more serious or fun-loving?"

"She's an old soul, but she knows how to have fun."

Sasha nodded. "The first one with the paisley comforter and matching abstract pictures is good. I also like the fourth one. The three tones of the accent pillows complement the forest-green bedspread." She handed the phone back to him.

A room for Mackenzie would make his apartment feel more like home.

After pushing 6282R into the hangar, Aubrey stood back in the drainage culvert for a moment to admire the beautiful airplane framed in the doorway. The day she met her Romeo came flooding back.

She had only been asleep for three hours after a grueling night shift. She had been working herself ragged taking on extra shifts to save for an airplane....and to forget.

Nate called and told her to meet him at hangar 55-3 right away. She wanted to fall back to sleep for about three days, but instead, she slugged back a 5-Hour Energy and drove to Deer Valley.

Her heart melted when she caught sight of a red, white, and blue V-tail. Nate introduced her to the former owner's widow, daughter, and son-in-law. He had passed away earlier that week, but the plane clearly had not been flown in years.

Nate pulled her aside and whispered, "How much do you have saved?"

"Around sixty grand. More if I liquidate some investments."

"It's going to need some work, and the family really wants it to go to someone who will appreciate it. I can probably talk them into an 'everyone's-happy' deal."

Her heart felt like it would burst while she could barely contain the butterflies in her stomach. "Let's do it."

She and Nate went to work on the deal. While Nate did most of the talking, Aubrey quickly memorized the N number. 6282 R for Romeo. Romeo. It was perfect. This was the only Romeo she would ever need.

After lowering her hangar door, Aubrey drove to Skyways and parked next to a green Kawasaki sport bike. She got out of her car and admired its lines. *This thing looks fast just sitting here.*

When she walked through the hangar, Ray came through the lobby door.

"Hey. Whose bike is that out there?"

"It's mine. Like it?" Daniel entered the hangar from the break room.

"Yeah. Will you take me for a spin on it?"

"I only have my permit, so I can't take passengers yet."

"No one will pull you over on the airport property."

He seemed to think this over for a moment. "Okay, but you wear my helmet."

She turned to Ray. "You still have the extra helmet here?"

He was beside her holding it. "Read both your minds."

Once Daniel was on the bike, she stepped up and swung herself onto the rear seat, bracing her hands against the tank. The bike's engine purred to life. He gently eased the clutch out and headed west in front of transient parking behind the main terminal. Once his feet were on his pegs, Aubrey leaned against him. They passed rows of single and twin-engine planes along with some jets. On the north side, one of AeroGuard's trainer planes was ready for takeoff on 7-Left while another was doing a run up.

Daniel was clearly a new rider, but he seemed to have a natural inclination. The solid feel of Daniel's back against her chest along with the vibration of the engine made the short excursion around the airport a thrill ride.

She took off the helmet before dismounting the bike. A heady mix of cologne, Fast Orange, sweat, and mechanic fluids wafted up into her nostrils. Aubrey took it all in for a second.

"Great bike. Thanks for the ride."

"Sure."

She caught a small glint in his eyes right as he turned the bike toward the exit gate.

Daniel rolled on and shifted the bike into second gear as he exited the airport. The light cool breeze brushed his arm hair and entered the slight opening in his visor. The turquoise and white of the FBI building was a blur in his peripheral as he turned left. Another click up with his right foot, a surge into third gear, and the engine sang.

He had always wanted a bike like this but felt they were too dangerous for a young father. Now his daughter was grown, and he had moved to a state with nearly year-round riding weather. No reason not to get his dream bike, a '17 ZX–6r.

Daniel's heart soared when the ZX seemed to grab the road on the long curve where 7th Street morphed into Happy Valley. He let out an unrestrained whoop!

Traffic caused him to roll back into second gear. He was sure Aubrey enjoyed the ride. In fact, her eyes showed a particular spark when she thanked him. The bike was heavier with her on the back, but he could get used to that. He would ride with her again with her breasts pressed against his back and her thighs straddling his.

Chapter Five

Aubrey headed up the walk toward Daniel's apartment. A woman with long, shapely legs accentuated by tight athletic shorts was standing at Daniel's door talking with him. Her hair in a high ponytail was a bronze, blonde, darker than Aubrey's. She turned when Daniel looked in Aubrey's direction. Her eyes were green, and she had a dusting of freckles across her nose and cheeks. Sweat dampened the front of her tank top and visible sports bra.

"Aubrey, I'll be ready in a second. By the way, this is my neighbor Rochelle." He turned to Rochelle. "Aubrey is a pilot at Deer Valley. She volunteers her plane for animal rescue flights."

"Impressive." Rochelle's eyes seemed to scan Aubrey.

The two women smiled and shook hands.

Daniel turned again to Rochelle. "Thank you. I'm sure I can be there." He then disappeared inside, leaving the front door open.

"Nice meeting you, Aubrey. I'm going to finish my run. Hope the dog works out."

"Nice meeting you too."

Rochelle turned and jogged down a cement path between two rows of multi-hued forest green, terracotta, and tan apartments. No jiggle in her tight butt.

"She seems nice," Aubrey said when Daniel emerged and locked his door.

"Yeah. She wanted to make sure I knew about the renter's meeting on Thursday night." They headed toward her car.

His tone seemed offhand, but she was sizing Aubrey up as competition. What did it matter anyway? Daniel was a friend. Just a friend. He and Rochelle were free to do whatever they wanted. Or not.

Daniel and Aubrey parked in front of a small house in a cookie-cutter neighborhood in Surprise.

While cleaning the belly of the Bonanza, he and Aubrey talked about her animal rescue activities. Throughout the years, Daniel had had various lab or shepherd mixes. His rental agreement did not have any pet restrictions as far as breed or size, but a large, active dog in an apartment didn't seem right. One small dog would add some sound, movement, and company. Better than the headaches of a roommate or the commitment and maintenance of a girlfriend. Aubrey was the first person he called about adopting a dog.

When she turned off her car, Aubrey looked at him. "Okay, I called in a favor for you to see this dog first because I really think he will be a good fit for you. Chiweenies are very popular, and he will find a home. If you don't think he's going to work out for you, say so. No hard feelings."

"Okay. Let's meet Briscoe and see what we think of each other."

When they entered the house, Daniel introduced himself to Connie, a woman in her early sixties. She led them to a small family room and told them to wait. Moments later, she came down the hall followed by a small, light tan, dog with long hair and semi-erect ears. As soon as the pup noticed them, he let out a small growl and hid behind his foster mother peeking out.

Connie glanced back at the pup. "It takes him a little time to feel safe. Once he realizes you are okay things will progress. We'll just ignore him and talk for a few minutes."

"Yes," Aubrey chimed in. "Like I said on the phone, Daniel is new to the state."

"That's right. How do you like it here?"

"There's a lot to like. The desert is beautiful. Also, I just bought a motorcycle which I understand I can enjoy most of the year."

"You can. But you'll never get me on one of those things." Connie shook her head.

Daniel chuckled. "Fair enough."

"Connie teaches junior high," Aubrey said.

"Really? I remember my daughter and her friends during that time. I never knew from one moment to the next what I'd be dealing with. A random traffic stop is more predictable."

Connie shrugged. "They have their moments. That's for sure. I guess I'm cut out for it."

Out of the corner of his eye, Daniel saw Briscoe slowly come out of hiding. He approached Aubrey.

She squatted down holding her hand out. "Hey you. You remember me don't you, boy?"

Briscoe wagged his tail in response.

Daniel lowered himself to the area rug that covered part of the laminate floor. The little dog cocked his head and slowly approached him, sniffing. He continued sniffing as he climbed into Daniel's lap and placed his front paws on his chest. Daniel slowly moved his hand up toward the dog's nose to be further sniffed. The dog skittered away with a small yip.

"Hey. Sorry buddy. I won't do that anymore, okay? It's alright." Daniel leaned against the sofa and placed his hands in his lap. The dog slowly approached him again. After a moment, Daniel moved one finger to gently scratch the dog's chest. The pup tensed for a quick moment but did not skitter away.

The older woman turned to Aubrey. "Why don't you and I go into the kitchen and let them get further acquainted."

Aubrey and Connie caught up over iced tea at the small hexagonal table in Connie's breakfast nook. Aubrey stole glances into the family room. The rescue dog was getting visibly more comfortable. Before long, the chiweenie was settled against Daniel's chest. The finger scratching was replaced by his whole hand running down the length of the dog's body.

By the time Aubrey finished her tea, Connie finished a story of the latest drama in her classroom. Daniel came in carrying Briscoe. The once nervous pup looked like Daniel's arms were where he had been all his life. He wagged his fluffy tail when he laid eyes on Connie and Aubrey.

Daniel fished his phone out of his pocket. "Can one of you take our picture? I want to introduce Mackenzie to her new brother."

Aubrey opened the borrowed locker in the break room at the Maricopa County Medical Center. The Friday night shift in the ER was finally over, and she was ready to go home, make some eggs and toast, then catch some Z's.

She took her phone out of her purse to find a Facebook Messenger attachment from her mother featuring three different styles of bouquets. She sent her opinion on them. Next, she saw a text from her friend Sam asking if she was free that Friday night. *Nope*. Another text came in from Daniel sharing a picture of Briscoe curled up on a dog bed with a couple of toys on the floor in front of him.

He's settling in really well. I hope your shift wasn't too dramatic. I remember how crazy weekend night shifts can be.

She texted back a smiling face with hearts emoji.

Good to hear. Some drama, but not too much.

Lastly, she saw that she had a voicemail from her father. She hadn't heard from him since he left the note on her windshield at Civil Air Patrol over a month ago.

She took her remaining belongings out of the locker and made her way past several round tables toward the exit.

What was she going to do about the message? Play or delete? Play or delete? What the hell did he want? He couldn't be wondering what was going on with her. Along the same lines, it couldn't be about a family member. She and her mother kept in contact with both sides of the family. That left him wanting to tell her something regarding himself. He probably found himself a trophy wife who thought the money would be worth putting up with him. If that were the case, she didn't need to hear about it.

She reached the employee section of the parking garage. Once in the driver's seat, she turned her phone over in her hand a few times. She moved her thumb to the delete button, then rolled her eyes and hit play instead.

"Aubrey, I know you don't want to talk to me and that's fine. If you'll give me a moment, we can talk, and I'll leave you alone after that."

She looked at her phone. 7:20 a.m. He'd be up. Still, she wasn't going to call him just because he wanted her to. How many years had she done his bidding? For the first twelve years of her life, she was the perfect Daddy's girl always making him look like Father of the Year. When her teen years hit, she started having her own ideas about who she was. And who she wanted to be. He couldn't have that, so he clamped down. She rebelled. At sixteen, she acquiesced enough to keep him calm and bided her time until her eighteenth birthday.

She hit the delete button.

Chapter Six

Aubrey pulled into the parking lot of Thunderbird Conservation Park and parked next to her mom's Prius. A cool breeze greeted her when she exited her jeep. The two women embraced bumping the bills of their ball caps, laughing before heading to the trailhead.

"Mom, Dad's been trying to contact me. Do you know anything about that?"

"No. You know I don't talk to him."

Mother and daughter hiked up the first small hill in silence. The park was an expanse of rocks and boulders in every shade of gray and tan nestled among every shade of green. Imposing saguaros towered over creosote and ocotillo bushes. Smaller barrel and prickly pear cacti rounded out the beauty of the desert fall morning.

"How's Charlie doing?" Aubrey asked.

"He's great. Since we're keeping the wedding simple, there's not a lot for him to do...or me, for that matter."

They moved aside at the bell of a mountain biker coming up the hill behind them.

"Low stress, no drama. Sounds ideal."

Her mother smiled and nodded. Aubrey's heart swelled seeing her mother so happy. Loraine met Charlie, a widower, when he moved into her community three years ago. Their friendship slowly blossomed into love. Now their wedding was fast approaching.

"For the sake of the planning, will you be bringing someone?"

"Probably. I'm sure someone will be available. Whether I come alone or with someone, there will always be questions."

"They want you to be happy."

A lizard skittered across the path.

"I am happy. I have 6282 Romeo. He's enough for me."

"Yeah, don't you two go dying together. Okay?"

Daniel packed up his Smith and Wesson 9mm pistol on the counter of his and Roger's lane at the shooting range. He then holstered his Glock 19. C2 Tactical in Scottsdale was a good place to meet as it was near Roger's house and a short drive on Loop 101 for Daniel. Roger, now a Sheriff's Deputy for Maricopa County, had influenced Daniel's decision to move to Arizona.

Carrying their respective pistol cases, they nodded toward the Range Safety Officer.

"You guys have a good day." The young man with dark red hair and glasses smiled.

When they exited the two sets of doors from the range into the brightly lit store, they approached the counter to collect their driver's licenses. Daniel placed his Glock in its appendix-carry position in his right front pocket.

Sonja, the manager, beamed when she handed Daniel his license. "How'd you do?" Her fingers brushed his hand slightly.

"Done better, done worse."

He held her gaze for a long moment. She didn't look away, only secured a strand of dark hair behind her ear.

Once in the parking lot, Roger stopped before turning toward his car. "You know, you should come here without me and see what kind of conversation develops. Those dark eyes spoke volumes."

"Maybe, but right now, I think another set of deep brown eyes will want me to take him to the park when I get home."

As he got into his Ram, Daniel had an idea. He pulled out his phone and sent a text to Aubrey.

Do you have a recommendation for a good dog park?

Aubrey met Daniel at Deer Valley Park. In the early evening, three of the four expansive, grassy enclosures were busy with dogs of varying sizes, breeds, and mixes. She found Daniel in the small-dog enclosure sitting on a bench watching Briscoe run around with some other mixed breeds.

"Got your text that you decided to come here. Hope you don't mind me just showing up."

"No. I'm glad you came. I like the dog park in my complex, but this is a nice change of pace. Nice to have an area just for small dogs."

They sat in silence for a few moments watching Briscoe.

Daniel's phone rang. Aubrey now recognized the crickets as Mackenzie's ring tone.

"Hey there.... Whoa, what's wrong!?"

Uh oh. Aubrey got up from the bench and walked a few feet away to give Daniel some privacy. She picked up a tennis ball and threw it. Briscoe and several others ran after it. A few words floated in her direction. Daniel's tone was concerned, and he appeared to be problem-solving with his daughter.

After throwing several balls and toys, she heard Daniel end the call and rejoined him on the bench.

"Everything okay?"

"Yeah. Mac stayed out too late, then overslept and missed an important test. Prof. won't let her retake it. Looks like she's going to have to bust her butt doing extra credit to replace the lost points."

"So, she majorly screwed up and she calls you?"

Daniel tilted his head and shrugged. "Yeah. Me or her mother. I'm a little more objective than Jen, so I would be the logical first call in that situation."

Aubrey shook her head. "When I messed up, my father was the last person I would call. The mistakes he did find out about were met with long lectures centered around how the mistake made him look and feel."

Daniel shrugged again. "She's going to mess up sometimes. She's a young woman finding her way in life. My hope is that she learns from her mistakes and that they aren't too catastrophic."

Aubrey slowly shook her head. "So, her missing that test is not about you?"

"From the moment we found out Jen was pregnant, things were not about me. I remember the night we graduated high school. Our friends were having or going to graduation parties. We had to go home and put our four-month-old to bed."

Aubrey smiled at him and nodded. At that moment, Briscoe ran up and sat in front of them dropping a ball at Daniel's feet. He got up and threw the ball, laughing as he watched his dog and others run after it. Aubrey's heart melted while warmth flooded her. Seemingly out of nowhere, her stomach tightened. *Take your time. Keep getting to know him. Remember the last one.*

Fear Farm was less crowded on a weeknight than on most weekends. Daniel looked across the parking lot toward the dilapidated structures and the sinister sign above the entrance. Giant skeletons and aliens sat high above the fence looking down on the scene with glowing eyes. The sounds of chainsaws and screams emanated from behind the gates.

Aubrey grabbed his hand and looked down at his feet. "I see you knew to wear running shoes."

He laughed. "Mackenzie and I used to go to things like this all the time. I think I like Halloween events because I know it's not real so I can just enjoy it and not feel like I need to take care of the situation."

"Makes sense." She grabbed his hand and led him to the ticket window.

After buying their tickets, they entered the fray of characters and guests. They walked in front of a porch with an open door where blood-spattered walls and a flickering television adorned the inside. A woman with a pig mask and faded flowered dress stood on the porch holding up what looked like raw meat.

"Do stay for dinner," she said, then cackled.

"We'll take a rain check," Aubrey called out, then stopped and looked up at an airplane lodged in the roof of another house. "That is actually terrifying."

"You think it's real, like from a salvage yard?" he asked.

"I'm sure it is."

Behind them, they heard the clatter of a chainsaw. A man with open wounds, scars and torn clothing was gaining on them. Aubrey screamed and ran. Daniel followed. Aubrey ran one direction, then as soon as they turned a corner, she raced toward a barn. Her eyes were aglow, her skin flushed.

"This way!" her voice barely above a whisper as she led him behind a wall of hay bales.

Once he turned the corner, he stumbled, pushing Aubrey against the hay. Instead of righting himself immediately, he stood against her looking into her eyes. Her hyperventilation brushed his cheek. He tipped his head toward her, bringing his lips almost to hers.

The high pitched, maniacal scream of a clown with an ax caused them to startle and run. Within moments, they were back in the fray.

Later that evening, Daniel walked toward his apartment. Damn that clown. Then again, maybe he did Daniel a favor.

Running footsteps behind him caused him to spin around, heart pounding. Rochelle, face flushed and out of breath, ran toward him carrying Rufus.

"Rochelle! What's wrong?"

"Daniel. I need you!"

Chapter Seven

Aubrey came up Daniel's walk carrying a dog bed, crate, and a bag of treats. After working with Briscoe, she might suggest they go to dinner. The evening was cooling off now that it was November, but they could still take Briscoe and eat outdoors.

Daniel's door opened. Aubrey stopped where she was. Rochelle, the woman who had been at his door around a month ago, walked out with a Papillon on a leash beside her. They were laughing over something. This time, her gorgeous figure was clad in a forest green pullover and navy slacks. Her long hair fell down her back and chest.

What the hell is she doing here? How often is she here?

Daniel smiled when he saw her. "Hey, Aubrey. Thanks for bringing everything." He met her halfway and took the items from her. "I got the shredded mess of his other bed cleaned up."

"Nice to see you again, Aubrey. This is my Rufus." Rochelle bent down and picked up her dog.

The fluffy dog wagged its tail when Aubrey petted him. "You're a baby, aren't you, Rufus? Yes, you are...He's adorable."

Rochelle smiled a genuine, warm smile that Aubrey couldn't help but return.

"So is Briscoe. He's perfect for Daniel despite the little oops this evening."

"I had a hunch, and my hunches are usually right."

Rochelle turned back toward Daniel's open door. "See you later, Daniel," she called into the apartment. "You too, Aubrey, I'm sure."

Aubrey waved as Rochelle turned down the sidewalk between gravel lawns accented with sage bushes. She then entered the apartment. Once inside, she scanned the open floor plan for evidence of dinner or drinks for two but found none.

Daniel turned from his kitchen holding a plate of cookies out to her. "Want a cookie? Rochelle brought them over as a thank you. I got a spider out of her bathroom last week. Apparently, she's terrified of spiders."

Oh Eek! A spider! Daniel, come save me. It's got eight legs. I'm so scared!

"Aubrey...Cookie?"

Daniel stood before her with a quizzical look. He moved the plate toward her. "Oh. Yes, thank you." She took a cookie off the plate. *Get a grip!*

Daniel set the plate down on the quartz countertop, took the bed and crate from the floor and headed down the short hallway toward his bedroom.

The flavors of chocolate chips and dried cranberries blended together beautifully. What was her problem anyway? Rochelle seemed very nice. It appeared she loves animals. Besides, a lot of people are afraid of spiders. She had no claim on Daniel and didn't want to commit to anyone anyway. He and Rochelle could have dinner, drinks, or several plates of cookies for all it mattered.

Daniel merged onto the Loop 101 toward McQueen Field where his team, the Monsoons, would play that Friday evening. He hadn't realized when he joined the adult leagues that he'd make frequent trips all the way out to Gilbert. Then again, it wasn't until Nate sent him on a few parts runs out there that the term East Valley made sense. Deer Valley Airport was considered North Valley. His phone rang the chirping crickets.

"Hey Mac! You wrapping up classes for another week?"

"Yep. I went to the Gallogly Center for a swim, and later a few of us are going to a movie. Thought I would check in with you in between. What are you doing?"

"Heading to a game. We're playing against the Valley Cats tonight."

You guys beat the Cats last time, right?

"Yeah, we'll do it again tonight."

"Text me later and let me know the score."

Mackenzie seemed distracted by voices.

"Well, I gotta go. Love you."

Daniel had to marvel at Mackenzie. She busted her butt to get a full scholarship. Now she was maintaining excellent grades while enjoying a whirlwind social life. Friends, outings, and a date or two.

Good for you Mac. Grab it with both hands.

He had been in the running for a baseball scholarship to the University of Providence when his life took its detour. Yes, he became a dad before he was ready and as a result grew up too fast. Like most young parents, though, he now had the rest of his life ahead of him. For many years, he figured he would remarry and have another child or two like Jen and Wyatt did. The older Mackenzie got, the less interested he was in starting the whole parenting thing over again. His last relationship ended in a perfect storm. Mac was in high school, he was feeling the pull to get out of law enforcement, and his girlfriend was ready to start a family. He then realized how much he didn't want to start over with another child. Both Rochelle and Aubrey hadn't had children but were still young enough to do so. Potential problem. Sonja was a little older than him and had two teenagers. She could still want to start a second family. How would any of them respond to his being one-and-done with Mackenzie?

Daniel parked near the baseball diamonds at the sprawling park and grabbed his duffle bag out of the back seat of the Ram. *Take it slowly, Daniel, now's your time to grab life with both hands.*

The second Tuesday of the month always came quickly. When Aubrey arrived at the conference room on the second floor of the Deer Valley Terminal, Bob was the only one there. *Great.*

The fifty-something ex-airshow pilot leaned back in his chair. "How's the cute girl pilot this evening?"

She met and held his eyes without a word and began setting out the plates, napkins, and cups she brought for the Deer Valley Pilot's Association Board Meeting.

He leaned back in his chair and brushed some of his fading blonde hair off his forehead. "You know, you really missed out not going to Sedona with me back in July. The weather was great that weekend. Not that there was a lot of outdoor activity, mind you."

Aubrey shrugged. "Like I said, you should have taken your wife."

He smirked. "You know, Aubrey, you won't always – "

"Hello, hello!" Ken walked in with a pink box from Crumbl Cookies.

Yeah. Yeah. I won't always look this good and have men chasing me. Oink. Oink. Have you seen yourself lately?

Aubrey took the box from Ken noting its weight. Ken's eyes met hers and twinkled. She gave him a small smile before setting the box on the table.

"Well Aubrey, I finally got Nate to agree to go golfing this Sunday."

"Well good. He works too much."

More members trickled in and took their places around the table.

"Looks like everyone is here." Ken motioned toward the pink box. "Please help yourselves."

Mike, the Association president, opened the box revealing a beautiful assortment of broccoli, cauliflower, peppers, grape tomatoes, and carrots. Almost everyone burst out laughing. A few people groaned.

Ken reached into a bag. "Okay, I know it wasn't what you all expected, but I brought some ranch dip and some of my wife's hummus."

"Ginny knows her way around garbanzo beans. That's for sure." Mike dished up a large helping along with some vegetables, then started the meeting.

Aubrey was just walking to her car after the meeting when her phone rang. Daniel's panicked voice shot through the phone. "Aubrey! It's Briscoe. I don't know what's wrong with him. Can you drive me to the nearest emergency vet?"

"I'll be right over."

Once she arrived, Aubrey opened the unlocked door. The stench of vomit and diarrhea assaulted her nostrils.

Daniel entered through the arcadia door leading from the patio with Briscoe in his arms. Some of the offensive fluids marked his shirt and pants. "He won't stop. It's coming out of both ends. I don't know what to do."

"How long?"

"The last few hours. He ate something on his walk before I could stop him."

She gently pulled on Briscoe's scruff. It did not bounce back right away.

"He's dehydrated from all the fluid loss. I need to call a friend. He's a vet tech." She dialed Sam's number.

Daniel was still holding Briscoe when Aubrey left. He dropped onto his sofa. She returned moments later with a bald man in his late 20's carrying an IV tower and bag.

Daniel had cleared his coffee table and put three layers of towels on it as instructed. He now laid Briscoe on the towels.

Aubrey's friend, Sam, set the tower by the coffee table, attaching the bag and tube to it.

"Hey, boy. You don't look so hot. I got something to help you feel better." He turned to Aubrey. "He appears to be about 15 pounds, probably a little less due to dehydration." He then handed a pill to Aubrey. "Cut this in half."

"Sure." Aubrey headed for the kitchen.

"The knives are in the top drawer to the left of the stove." Daniel called out.

Sam was shaving Briscoe's front leg.

Minutes later Aubrey returned to the family room with half a pill coated with some olive oil. With quick movements, she opened his dog's mouth, put the pill in, and rubbed his throat.

By now, Sam had found a vein and inserted the IV needle. He ran his hand along the small dog's body. Briscoe turned listless eyes to Daniel, and his tail wagged slightly. Daniel melted into the cushions.

"Give him the other half of the pill in the morning. Aubrey can remove the IV in a few hours."

"Thanks for coming, man. I really appreciate it."

"No problem." Sam's glacial eyes held his for a moment. They seemed to question who he was to Aubrey.

Aubrey put a hand on Sam's back as she walked him to the front door.

Daniel awakened to Briscoe's wet nose and small licks to his chin.

"Hey you." He pulled the dog to his chest, cuddling him. "You scared the hell out of me last night."

Aubrey stirred and stretched from her reclining position on the couch beside him. "How is he?"

"Seems normal to me."

She sat up and looked him over. "He looks great."

Daniel's eyes met hers. "Thank you. For staying and all your help cleaning up."

"Of course." She got up and headed for the hall bathroom.

"How do you like your eggs?" Daniel called out.

"Over medium."

A few minutes later, they sat down to eggs, toast, and half a pear each.

"I'll call my vet after breakfast to see if I can get Briscoe in today. Do you think Nate will be okay with me bringing him to work? I don't want to leave him alone today."

"He'll let you. He knows he'll have me to deal with if he doesn't."

Daniel laughed. Why did his home feel so much more complete with her in it? He was finally on his own and happy. Yet often it seemed he wanted to bring someone else in. Not just anyone - her. Of course, there was also the vet tech who came over last night. Were they an item? Judging from what others had said about Aubrey, probably not.

Aubrey entered the curtained-off room at Banner Children's Urgent Care. A 9-year-old Hispanic boy leaned against his mother. Tears streamed down his face. His left arm was bloodied with a line of road rash from his shoulder to his elbow. What was once a short sleeve shirt now resembled jagged ribbons. Poor guy.

"Oh my, Daniel, that has to hurt."

The boy nodded as fresh tears coursed down his cheeks.

"Maybe he'll think about this next time he and his friends try to out-do each other on their bikes," the father said.

"By the way, his name is Donelo," the mother corrected.

Aubrey looked at the chart for a second. "Yes, that's right. Well, Donelo, I'm afraid this won't be comfortable, but it needs to be done to protect you from infection. Okay?"

The boy nodded. More tears trickled down his cheeks.

As gently as she could, Aubrey rinsed and removed bits of asphalt and pebbles until only badly scraped skin remained. She then applied Lidocaine and bandages.

"You were very brave Dan...Sorry, Donelo.

After instructing the parents on how to care for their son's wound, Aubrey left the room for her next patient. A few steps out the door, she heard the mother say, "Boy, someone named Daniel is on her mind."

It was true. She couldn't get Daniel off her mind. His chiseled features, his unusual eyes, the way he clearly kept his body in shape all stirred her senses. But there was also the sound of his laugh, and how easy it was to talk to him. She truly wanted to be around him. Truly liking someone was a requirement for her. Problem was, her friends-with-benefits relationships worked well because she kept all of her friends in different sectors of her life. She already had an FWB at the airport, albeit an infrequent friend. Still, he was one she was not willing to give up. She had already broken one of her rules by having Sam come over to help Daniel with Briscoe the other night. Having two of them in the same room was not done. However, Daniel was not an FWB. Not yet, anyway. So really, the rule was not broken. Even so, getting sexually involved with Daniel was probably a bad idea. He worked at Skyways, after all. Was he even open to an FWB arrangement in the first place?

Chapter Eight

When Daniel entered the Skyways hangar, Nate was working at his desk in his back corner office. He looked up from his paperwork through the plexiglass and smiled, motioning for Daniel to come in.

Nate handed Daniel a flier. "I'm sure you have seen these around the airport lately."

"Yeah, I'm familiar with the Young Eagles program. Some of the airports in Montana put on events, usually during the spring and summer."

"Well, for obvious reasons, we do ours in November. Skyways usually has a volunteer or two at the yearly event. I'll be one of the pilots, so will Aubrey, but I wondered if you would like to represent us on the ground this year."

"Sure. My daughter took a Young Eagles' flight. It's a great program."

Nate gave him a thumbs up. "Okay. I'll see you at Cutter on Saturday morning."

Deer Valley Airport was bustling on Young Eagles' Day. Parents, grandparents and children flitted among the tables decorated with signs and balloons. Cutter Aviation across the terminal from Skyways always hosted the Experimental Aircraft Association's event. Aubrey always planned for the day off in advance so she could take children on their first general aviation flight. It was through Young Eagles at the age of twelve that she was introduced to her first love.

Often, she relived the day when an EAA member had brought her and two younger children to an orange and white Cessna 172. The volunteer named Jack introduced them to the pilot named Matt, a heavy-set man with white hair. The butterflies in her stomach felt like they would break free. Aubrey motioned for the other two to get into the back seat and jumped into the front beside the pilot. She took a breath to calm herself since her parents had told her to be polite. From the first take off, Aubrey was hooked. The freedom of flying so high above the neighborhoods and deserts was like nothing she had felt before. Seeing her town of Carefree from so high up was amazing. The brother and sister behind her chattered a mile a minute. Aubrey, however, took a keen interest in everything the pilot did. He seemed to have picked up on her curiosity and began explaining what he did and what the gauges were for. Then came the moment she would never forget: the moment he let her fly the plane. The fluttering in her stomach disappeared. Her world consisted of only Matt's instructions and what the plane did in relation to the controls. Those few moments changed her life forever. It was then that she knew she wanted to fly more than anything else in the world. She instinctively threw her arms around Matt in a big hug before she exited the plane. Today, just like at other events, she would give children the gift that Matt had given her.

The day flew by in a blink. After getting pictures with her last group of passengers and their parents, she saw Daniel heading toward her. His black shirt with 'Young Eagles Volunteer' in white letters across the front accentuated his chest and arms. When he reached her, he leaned in and lowered his voice. "A family arrived and signed in late. We said we weren't sure if we could fit their daughter in. Would you be willing to take her up?"

She looked past Daniel's shoulder toward a Black family. The girl looked to be about eight years old. "I'll never leave a Young Eagle on the ground."

Daniel motioned them over. "Aubrey, this is Reylon."

"Reylon, nice to meet you." Aubrey held out her hand.

The girl smiled shyly and shook her hand.

She then shook hands with Reylon's parents. "Would one or both of you like to go up with her?"

Her father held up a hand. "No, that's okay."

The mother shook her head but smiled. "We're here because Reylon's teacher had a guest speaker who flies these little airplanes. Now it's all she talks about. It took us up to the last minute to decide to sign her up."

"I understand." Aubrey turned back to the girl who was practically dancing on the tarmac. "Ready for your first flight?"

The Young Eagle nodded and beamed at her.

As they walked to the plane, Aubrey heard Daniel talking with the girl's parents. "Aubrey's an excellent pilot." The conversation faded, but the reassuring tone remained.

Aubrey brought Reylon to the Bonanza's wing and explained that the black textured section was the only part strong enough to walk on. She helped the young girl up onto the wing then buckled in herself and her charge.

"Clear," she said after following the hot-start procedure, expelling vapor from the fuel lines and turning the ignition on. The girl beamed again.

Using the rudder pedals, she turned onto the taxiway. "We are now taxiing to the runway. Taxi is when the plane moves on the ground. See, I'm using the rudder pedals to steer the plane the way I want it to go."

The girl moved sideways to watch Aubrey turn the plane right then left.

"When we're in the air, I'll be using these pedals and the steering wheel, which is called the yoke, to make the plane turn. I'll even let you do it if you want to."

"Yes," she said, speaking to Aubrey for the first time.

After doing and explaining the run up, Aubrey taxied to the runway. "Deer Valley Tower, Bonanza 6282 Romeo ready for takeoff on 25 Left."

"Bonanza 82 Romeo cleared for takeoff."

"82 Romeo cleared for takeoff." The two were in the air.

When Aubrey helped Reylon down from the wing 30 minutes later, she saw Reylon's smiling parents approaching.

"How was your flight?" her mother asked.

"It was great!" Reylon answered.

The parents exchanged a look full of mixed emotions.

Reylon's mom turned to Aubrey. "Thank you. We very much appreciate you flying with her."

"Sure. We need more young women in aviation."

The father gave a slight cringe.

They all took some pictures by the plane, then went to the table for Reylon to collect her certificate and wings.

Aubrey and Daniel helped the Cutter Aviation crew clean up and shut down the popular event. When Aubrey pushed her plane into her hangar, her phone rang. *Daniel.*

"I'm a little homesick today," he said. "The Q Bar and Grill reminds me of some of the restaurants in Montana. Would you like to join me?"

Daniel had gone home to let Briscoe out, so when he arrived, Aubrey was already there sitting in a booth. A goose taxidermized in full flight adorned the wall above her. Her beautiful smile greeted him across the room while the jukebox played "Lady" by Styx. He crossed the room as if magnetically drawn to the table.

"Sorry you're missing home tonight," she said when he sat across from her.

"It happens. I'm still glad to be here. Mostly I miss Mackenzie right now. She had midterms this week, so we didn't talk much."

The server appeared with Aubrey's soda asking Daniel for his drink order. "Coke or Pepsi please."

"It couldn't have been easy with you and your ex being teen parents."

"Oh, it wasn't." Daniel shook his head. "Fortunately, our high school had on-site childcare, and we had supportive families on both sides, so we were able to graduate."

"Good."

"After high school, Jen started community college, and I worked as a records technician for the Great Falls Police Department. I remember one night, or early morning I should say, Mackenzie woke up at 3:00

in the morning and would not go back to sleep. Five o'clock rolled around with no settling in sight. I had work. Jen had classes. We realized the bakery down the street had just opened. I looked at how much money I had and knew I would get paid the next day, so we bundled Mackenzie up and had breakfast at the bakery, which included strong coffee."

"Let me guess, as soon as she was under the care of someone else, she went right down."

"That's right. Grandma arrived, and she conked right out."

He smiled at the memory while putting ranch dressing onto his salad. "What about you? I know you're not married, and I have never seen you at the airport with kids you call your own. Although a lot of them seem to know and love you."

"Yeah, I'm Aunt Aubrey to a lot of the airport kids. You're right, I'm on my own, and I'm good with that." Her eyes hardened with the defensiveness he had often seen during traffic stops.

So I've heard.

"Okay. What about your parents?"

"My dad lives in a nice house on a half-acre in Carefree. He and his business partner have owned and sold several successful businesses. Everything they touch turns into money. As a result, he lives by the Golden Rule."

"He who has the gold makes the rules?"

"That's the one. I've seen him a couple of times at family events, but I haven't talked to him in years."

His heart sank a little. *That explains a few things.*

"And your mom?"

"She got tired of having to make him look good and finally left." Aubrey dipped a fry in some ketchup. "After that, we rebuilt our relationship. She lives in a nice 55+ community in Scottsdale. When she left, and he couldn't convince her to come back, he knew she could take him for half of everything. He couldn't have that." She rolled her eyes. "So they and their lawyers worked out an investment plan. She gets a more than reasonable amount of money per month for the rest of her life. She's now happily engaged."

Daniel entered his apartment and released Briscoe from his crate. Tail going a mile a minute, he bounced, hitting his paws against Daniel's shins. Daniel's heart swelled at the joy of the little dog. All he had to do was walk in the door, and this was the response.

"Alright. I know I'm a little late feeding you. Sorry." He scooped the dog food Aubrey had recommended into Briscoe's bowl.

Aubrey had some red flags Daniel couldn't shake. She was fiercely independent and seemed to have a lot of male friends. Then there was the broken relationship with her father. His heart twisted. He had felt the sting of judgement as a teen father divorced by twenty. Now he was judging her.

For a time, the women his age he tried to date didn't want to deal with a child and an ex-wife. Of course, as he got older, the women themselves were often divorced single parents, so dating got easier.

Dating? Who said he would date Aubrey? She was a friend, a good friend with a good heart. She had made a real difference in his adjustment to a new state. Right now, a friend was all she needed to be.

Chapter Nine

The main strut repair Daniel had been assigned turned into an overtime affair. Everyone else had gone home two hours ago. Ricardo offered to stay and help him finish, but he declined the offer since Ricardo's wife Gabrielle had recently given birth to their third child. The others all had commitments that evening. Daniel relaxed his jaw from its clenched position. Maybe time to call it a night?

Suddenly, he heard a key unlock the side door of the hangar. Aubrey entered the hangar carrying a bag from Mr. Goodcents. Briscoe ran up to greet her, standing on his back paws, sniffing the air.

"No, baby. This isn't for you, but I brought you a treat."

Her eyes met his. "May I? She held up a morsel."

Daniel nodded. "Anytime."

The fluffy dog's tail whipped back and forth when Aubrey gave him the treat. Knowing Aubrey, it would have only the best ingredients.

"Nate said you were stuck on a main-strut repair. Thought you might be hungry. Ready for a break?"

"Am I ever!" His stomach growled as his mood lightened.

They made their way around the Cessna 182 Ray had been working on to the break room where Aubrey unpacked an eight-inch turkey sub for herself and a sixteen-inch Italian for him. He would probably need a Pepto Bismal tablet or two tonight. Roast beef and clubs were more his style, but it was easy to see why she thought he would like an

Italian. Daniel got out two of his sodas from the fridge, then put one back when he saw that she had a large can of Arizona Iced Tea.

They took a few moments to enjoy their sandwiches in silence.

"So, what brings you here from the beauty of Montana?"

"Well, first of all, in the winter it's not so beautiful. The place is a meat locker a good portion of the year. One of my fellow troopers moved here after his wife got a job in Phoenix. I went to visit him for a week one February, and I decided I would retire out here."

"You retired from the force this early?"

She took off her jean jacket, drawing his eyes to the faded T-shirt with the word Beech and a V-tail airplane across the front. He quickly looked at her face.

"No, I knew my time in law enforcement was up. I still wanted to work outdoors, but not in construction. I had been around airports a fair amount, and I've always been mechanically inclined, so I thought being an A and P was a good fit. I worked things out financially and went to trade school."

"And here you are. I'm figuring you're here because your daughter is now eighteen and no longer living in Montana, so you are free to live wherever you want."

"Yeah. I wouldn't have left her. Jen and I living within a two-hour drive from each other was part of the joint custody agreement. Truth is, we almost always lived within a few miles of each other, making it easier to raise Mac together."

Aubrey nodded. "So, is there a woman back home pining for you?"

He shook his head. "My last relationship ended about three years ago. Soon after, I was busy with trade school, waiting tables, and raising a teen daughter. Then I decided to move here. Another relationship didn't seem to fit in. Right now, I'm enjoying getting to know people here."

Daniel got up to get scissors out of a drawer to help Aubrey open a second mustard packet. "Speaking of getting to know people. I've been wondering why you chose nursing over flying professionally."

"The short answer is, I didn't want my love to become a chore. You have to work a lot of hours for low pay before you can make any real money flying. Then there's the dynamic of fly here, fly there, take off at this time, land at that time. With fill-in nursing, I knew I could work flexible hours and earn a good living."

She doesn't do much on others' terms. "Makes sense. I'd better get back to work."

Aubrey stood up. "Come on. Let's show that strut who's boss."

Stomach burning, Daniel popped the Pepto Bismal tablets he knew he'd need in order to sleep.

Aubrey had turned his rough day completely around. The repair he thought would take several more hours was done in record time. Of course, being under the nose with her made the time seem faster than it was. Even in an old T-shirt, she was beautiful. After the repair was in the plane's airframe log, they walked Briscoe in the gravel yard in front of Skyways. Right about the time his stomach started to burn, she wrapped him in a friendly hug, and they parted ways.

Warmth radiated from his chest to his groin. If tonight was any indication, they may be good partners in many areas. *Tread carefully with that one,* Ray's warning came back in a rush, repeating in his mind.

After a successful Civil Air Patrol flight, Aubrey stopped off at Sky-ways to hang out near closing time. When she made her way to the hangar, she found Ricardo's wife Gabrielle laughing with Justine. Newborn Elena Isabella was cradled in Justine's arms. Ricardo's five- and seven-year-old sons were in the corner near Nate's office with Briscoe. The fluffy dog wagged his tail and licked the boys' hands while being petted. Ricardo was looking on. *Good.*

Aubrey went over to Justine and Gabrielle. The infant's rosebud mouth was making sucking motions in her sleep. "Oh my! She's beautiful. Not that there was any doubt." She smiled at Gabrielle.

"All my kids get their looks from their mama," Ricardo called to Aubrey.

The third-time mom beamed at her husband.

"She also looks very healthy." Aubrey stroked the newborn's head above the lace headband.

"Doctor says she's doing great," Gabrielle said.

Briscoe was now getting tummy rubs from the two boys.

At that moment, Daniel emerged from the break room. "Come on, Big B. Let's go home."

Briscoe turned right-side up and trotted over to Daniel.

Aubrey walked over to the little group at what was now known as Briscoe's Corner. "What did you do to this dog anyway, Daniel? He's nothing like the dog we picked up at Connie's house."

"Well, you said he was fearful, so I looked into the best way to so-cialize a fearful dog. I also got some one-on-one sessions with trainers from PetSmart. I've been taking it slowly."

Slowly with quick results.

He put a hand on the shoulder of each boy. "I know these boys have excellent manners, so they were the first kids I introduced him to."

The boys beamed with pride.

Aubrey locked her car in the employee garage a little before seven in the morning. She turned and was stopped in her tracks. *Chad.*

"Well. Hello there, Aubrey."

Her face fell. Dr. Chad Hartshorn still had his tousled, sandy curls, but they now had flecks of gray throughout. More lines on his face than he had had seven years ago, but he looked less tired and more rugged than he did as a surgical resident.

"Chad. Are you here on business?"

"No, my divorce became final recently, and I decided Houston was no longer the place for me. I renewed my rights in all of the Arizona hospitals, and here I am." He opened his arms pulling his button-down shirt across his broad chest.

"I don't want to be late for my shift." She turned on her heel toward the ER's breakroom. Her heart hammered while she willfully kept her gait calm.

Daniel fired his Smith and Wesson four times, then nodded approvingly. The door from the antechamber whispered open. Sonja walked in carrying a target which she taped to the cardboard in the lane next to his. After sending the target out five yards, she whipped the side arm off her hip and emptied the magazine.

"Nice," Daniel said when he saw the cluster of bullet holes.

He then finished off his magazine.

"You too." Her brown eyes sparkled when they met his. "Hang on. I'll be right back."

She returned a moment later with two targets. The Range Safety Officer smiled, suppressing a laugh.

Sonja turned to Daniel. "Fifteen rounds rapid fire. Most in the center wins."

"What are we playing for?"

She took in her bottom lip and appeared to think it over. "One free range session for you. Margaritas at Blue Agave next door for me."

He inserted the magazine with a click. "You're on."

At the end of her shift, Aubrey found an envelope under her windshield wiper. She cringed. This never meant anything good. Especially after this morning. She glanced at the trash can near the building's entrance. *Hell.* She opened the envelope and pulled out a note. Chad Hartshorn's business card fell onto the ground. With a huff, she finished opening the note.

Aubrey,

I hate the way things ended between us. Let's at least talk.

Chad

She threw the note in a trashcan but left the business card on the ground.

The Blue Agave's cantina was a buzz of noise and activity around Daniel and Sonja's table.

"So how do you drink these? I mean, is there a proper way?" Daniel held up his margarita.

"First, lick a little salt from the rim. Then sip with your straw."

She demonstrated. The flick of her tongue on the rim and her lips around the straw sent a mild surge through him. Sonja had clearly applied fresh lipstick before meeting him at the Mexican restaurant.

Her eyes took him in as he followed suit. He suppressed a cough when the first splash of salt and tart citrus hit his tongue and throat.

"They take a little getting used to. Drink it slowly. By the way, thank you for meeting me for drinks anyway."

Daniel shrugged. "Well, I only beat you by two bullets. You're very good. Not only that, but I'm also trying to get to know more people in my new home state."

Her eyes lit up. "Your place or mine?"

Daniel sputtered his third sip and grabbed a napkin.

She burst out laughing. "Just kidding. Bad joke."

On her lunch break, Aubrey had called Carmella, her friend since Jr. high. The two made plans to meet that evening at LA Fitness where Carmella at times brought Aubrey as a guest. Outside the gym, they exchanged hugs. Aubrey relaxed against her for a moment taking in the familiar scent of Windows Down on her skin.

Carmella held her at arm's length, her deep brown eyes searching her face. "Hey. What's going on?"

She could hold back no longer, tears blurring Carmella's pink and black spandex. "He's back in Arizona."

"Oh no!"

"I guess his wife finally left him. Now he's back. Let's go work out. I'm so fucking pissed off!"

They entered the expanse of the main work out area. Music, weights clanging, and conversation melded into a cacophony. Aubrey headed for the lateral pull-down. She straddled the seat and grasped the bar. Carmella did the same on her lateral pull-down.

"He said his residency schedule gave us limited time together, and I believed him." She let out her breath, pulling the bar down to her chest.

While her pectorals tightened, each breath she forcibly exhaled released more tension. She turned around on the cushioned seat pulling the bar down behind her, inhaling on the way up, exhaling on the pull down. Her upper back and shoulders sang. *Come on. Two more.* She released the bar a little too early. A few members nearby turned and looked when the weights clanged together.

They walked over to the hamstring curl machine. Aubrey adjusted the weight by shoving the pin into the weight stack, this time not attracting any attention.

"He said he had a crash pad that he shared with another resident, so we never went to his place. Of course, I couldn't bring him to Nate and Justine's guest house, so we met in motel rooms and my car." She gripped the bars on each side of the seat. Tightening her abs, she slowly pushed down on the pad with her heels, exhaling.

When she slid off the seat, the backs of her thighs pulsed. She flexed and extended her complaining fingers.

Aubrey adjusted the pad downward and increased the weight to work her quadriceps, then slid back onto the seat. She reached for the bars again. *Okay. A little easier this time.* Memories of Chad's hands and lips on her body flashed through her mind as she counted out reps. Now the front of her thighs began to burn. She slowly let down the weights and sighed. The way he made her feel. Her previous partners had all been around her age and less experienced, as she had been. Chad knew where and how to touch. It had never been like that before.

She rose from the seat and shook her head at Carmella. "I guess all that oxytocin and dopamine made me stupid."

Carmella took the pink scrunchie from her wrist and tied back her thick black hair. "I keep telling you, Aubrey, you weren't stupid. You were in love."

"Is there a difference?"

Carmella flinched. "You know that I think so."

"Yes, and I'm thrilled you found Brock. I just don't see that happening for me."

The two friends headed for the free-weights and did sets of curls, triceps toners, and shoulder rolls in silence. It appeared that tonight, at least Carmella was going to spare Aubrey one of her pep talks on love. Her friend meant well, but the signs surrounding Chad might as well have been flashing neon.

Every exertion, every exhalation seemed to cleanse her. Now sweat soaked her black shorts and purple tank top while her arms trembled.

Aubrey sat down heavily on a bench while wiping her forehead with a towel. "You and Justine warned me. I didn't listen. Of course, you and Justine were the only people I talked to about the relationship since he said we had to keep it quiet. I had to have known and just chose to ignore it."

"Look. The only thing you're guilty of is being young and naive. We've all been there. He's getting his karma, and you're living life on your terms."

Aubrey nodded and looked up at her. "Smoothies?"

Carmella helped her up. "Let's go."

Chapter Ten

Aubrey had just left her hangar when Daniel, driving the fuel truck, pulled into her row of hangars stopping at the hangar on the corner.

Instead of getting into her car, she walked over to hangar 45-2. The direct sun overhead made her jean jacket over long sleeves unnecessary. Herman, in his characteristic Vietnam Vet hat, was just coming around his plane.

"Hey Herman. Are you getting ready for this year's toy drive for the Rez?"

"Yep. It officially starts Thanksgiving week."

"Well, you know you can count on me for some donations and hauling cargo."

"As always." He smiled and headed toward the restroom.

Daniel was ascending the ladder to unscrew the fuel cap on the Cessna 206, giving her an unobstructed view. *Love the way he fills out a pair of black Levi's.*

He looked over his shoulder.

She jerked her gaze to his face.

He gave a small smile and turned his attention back to the fuel cap.

"Looks like you drew the short straw today."

He chuckled and shrugged. "We all have to take our turn. Saw your car, I was going to come over to say hi. That is if you were there and not punching holes in the sky or saving the world's pets."

"Well, I'm glad you happened by. What are your plans for Thanksgiving?"

"I'm actually flying home. So is Mackenzie. It'll be nice to see everyone."

He climbed down the ladder and held her gaze for a moment on the way to retrieve the fuel nozzle. His lips turned in a cocky smile. Warmth rose to her cheeks and ears. *Hey, what do I have to feel guilty about? Guys do it all the time.*

"Sounds like it will be fun. Do you need someone to take care of Briscoe, or is he going with you?"

"I don't want to traumatize him with a commercial plane ride since I'll only be gone a few days. As I'm sure you've noticed, Sasha has fallen in love with him since I started bringing him to the airport."

"Yep. In fact, I'm starting to wonder who he really belongs to."

"Yeah. Me too. She's going to house sit and pet sit for me."

"That's great. How are you getting to the airport?"

"Uber, I figured."

Aubrey moved around the wing to face him. "Don't do that. How about I take you and pick you up?"

"That'd be great."

"Well, my motives aren't completely altruistic."

"Oh." Daniel laughed. "What do I need to do?"

"Be my plus-one at my mother's wedding this Saturday."

"Sure. Sounds like a fair-trade off."

"Be prepared for questions. My mother's side of the family has been wanting to see me married practically since I turned twenty." Aubrey rolled her eyes.

"Yeah, mine too. Every relationship since my divorce, my family hoped would be 'the one' and I would settle down and be happy."

"Were you unhappy between relationships?"

Daniel paused and gazed toward the roof. "I've had my ups and downs, but as a whole, not really. I have my daughter and my career. I have a good group of friends. I'm fine on my own."

Aubrey raised her chin and huffed. "Me too. It's not for anyone else to say."

A light fall breeze blew a few whisps of Aubrey's hair that had fallen out of its updo. She stood on the golf course to the right of the pastor with her mother's long-time friend Myra wearing their matching sage-green dresses. The day was perfect for an outdoor wedding. She smiled at Charlie. The dark-gray suit and silk tie set off his silver hair and trimmed mustache. He beamed back at her. The first couple of notes on the portable keyboard turned everyone's attention to the doorway of the Rio Rancho Clubhouse. Her mother, in an off-white suit, was every bit the classy, older bride coming down the aisle on the arm of Aubrey's Uncle Ian.

Aubrey teared up watching them exchange vows while looking into each other's eyes. Her heart wanted to burst and break at the same time. Would there ever be a man for her? One who loved her without wanting to own her? One who was as he appeared to be? Could a friendship turn into love? It seemed all of her FWB relationships were just that: friendships with sex on the side. Then there were her friendships with men that didn't involve sex. When she blinked away her tears, she looked toward Daniel who was focused on the ceremony. At the moment, Daniel was one of those friends. Over the years, Aubrey had attended several of her friends' weddings. Would she attend his too?

The marriage was sealed with the traditional kiss. It was now time to walk up the aisle on the arm of Charlie's brother, Ed. FOMO was not a reason to change the life she was mostly happy with. If she fell in love and committed to one man, it would have to be the right man for the right reasons.

Once up the aisle and in the event room, Ed kissed her hand and smiled. "It's not every day anymore that I have a beautiful young lady on my arm."

Daniel appeared beside her. Ed gave a nod to him and went to join his family and friends.

Aubrey led Daniel to the bride's family table where he took off his navy-blue sport coat.

"Hope that wasn't too boring for you."

"No, they seem really happy. It was a nice ceremony. I come from a tight-knit extended family, so there's always someone getting married or having a baby."

The afternoon flew by in a whirlwind of laughter and chatter. As the last slices of cake were served, guests made their way to the dance floor. Her mother and Charlie swayed together lost in each other. Her chest tightened. Would there ever be a moment like that for her – a day she would be so sure of someone that the idea of walking down the aisle was exhilarating rather than terrifying?

Aubrey leaned back in her chair feeling Daniel's warm presence beside her. She glanced at him while he watched the dance floor with a small smile.

"Maybe."

"What's that?" Daniel turned to her. His head tilted while his brow furrowed. "Hey. You okay?"

Realizing she had spoken aloud; heat rose to her face. "I'm great. I love seeing my mother so happy."

She stood up and held out her hand. "Come on. Let's dance."

The music shifted to something slow and soulful. Aubrey relaxed against him leaning her head against his shoulder feeling the steady rhythm of his heartbeat.

Maybe.

The evening was alive with the sounds of nocturnal insects and animals. After the wedding, Daniel and Aubrey changed clothes and picked up Briscoe. They took her Jeep up a winding path to a secluded mesa Aubrey had told him about.

Once they had exited the vehicle and found some even ground underneath a palo verde tree, they dug into the picnic dinner they picked up at Mr. Goodcents. Briscoe sniffed around for a few minutes, choosing a small boulder to lift his leg on before trotting over and curling up next to Daniel.

The sun was nearly at the horizon, causing the sky to explode in pink, yellow, and amber. Would he ever not notice the incredible sunsets? He took a glance at Aubrey. She seemed to be taking in the beauty while she sat close to him, slowly consuming her sandwich.

Briscoe stirred beside him. Aubrey reached over and petted him, leaning against Daniel to do so. She continued leaning on him after the petting session stopped.

He cautiously put an arm around her. She relaxed against his side.

"I've been wondering. You love animals, but you don't have a pet of your own. Why not?"

"I live alone and work long, unpredictable hours. I wouldn't want to leave a dog alone for hours on end. Then there's the need to let the dog out. I don't want to install a dog door because of coyotes."

"Yeah. I've seen them a time or two around my apartment complex."

"I guess no pets is one of the sacrifices I made for the life I chose."

She put her sandwich wrapping into its bag and relaxed further against him. "What was your first wedding like? Did you guys go all out or just go to the courthouse? If I'm being too intrusive, just say so."

"It's okay. When we found out Jen was pregnant, we had a week of full-scale freak-out. Neither one of us could concentrate on anything. We just went through the motions of our lives hoping no one would notice."

"How'd that go over?"

"Not well. We couldn't keep it up with our parents for long. They confronted us separately, then we met together to figure out what to do. We were very much in love and wanted our baby even though the timing wasn't right. There was no proposal, no bridal shower or bachelor party. The six of us simply agreed that Jen and I would get married and keep the baby."

Daniel shifted position. His arm around Aubrey was starting to tingle. *Damn.* She seemed to take his cue and turned to face him while leaning against a large rock.

"But you asked about the wedding itself," he continued. "We had a real wedding as soon as school let out our junior year. One of my uncles is a pastor, so he officiated. Jen's family lived on acreage, so we had a small, outdoor ceremony with our extended families and a few friends."

Aubrey held his gaze. Her eyes were shining, melting Daniel's heart.

Thanksgiving dinner was the same as always. The warmth of home and family enveloped Daniel. Everyone had gotten up early to cheer on Daniel's brother, niece, and nephew in the Burn the Bird 5K run. Now two turkeys and a fall centerpiece adorned the table along with his mother's mashed potatoes, his aunt's green beans, and other offerings brought by various family members.

Everyone was pulled in by Mackenzie's stories about college. She was animated while talking of new friends and experiences. His heart swelled. She was clearly thriving in the semi-adulthood of campus life. He caught up on the lives of his family members as they talked. When he shared details about his new life in Phoenix, some expressed envy at the high and low temperatures. It was cold this holiday weekend, but the real cold weather hadn't arrived yet.

After doing his part to help with the cleanup, he invited Mackenzie to go for a walk with him before she went for dessert at Jen's family gathering. Once outside, wearing their heavy fall jackets, beanies, and gloves, they walked in silence for a few minutes.

"I'm looking forward to your visits to Phoenix for New Years and spring break."

A gust of wind smelled of wet leaves and dirt. Mackenzie adjusted her bright green beanie.

"Me too. You said fall is really beautiful in Arizona. I bet winter and spring will be too." She stopped and turned to him. "Dad, I've been doing some thinking."

His heart quickened. *Thinking about what?*

"Should I be concerned?"

"No."

"Okay, what's on your mind?" *Just stay calm.*

She took a deep breath. "I know that I took up a lot of your life."

Daniel lifted his hands to chest level with his palms up.

"I know it wasn't my fault, and I know you don't regret having me. But you've started a new life in a new place. You now have a cute little dog and a motorcycle, so it seems like you're living for yourself now."

"I am."

"Then in your new life, I hope you will find someone to be happy with."

He took her hand and looked into her beautiful face. "I'm taking things very slowly, one day at a time."

"Good."

"In fact, I have a few new friends. One in particular. I'm not sure where it will go, but I'll be interested in what you think if you get to meet her in January."

She jumped up a down a few times, clapping her hands. "Either way, show me a picture and then tell me everything…Well, everything that's appropriate to tell me, anyway."

She laughed.

Daniel rolled his eyes, shook his head, and pulled out his phone.

Chapter Eleven

Aubrey woke up around 4:30 in the afternoon from a night shift. It was too quiet. When she got up and stretched, she pulled back her curtains to see low-hanging, dark clouds. *No flying today, and I did all my Christmas shopping on Cyber Monday...Skyways.*

When she walked into the lobby, Justine was on the phone and to her surprise, Daniel was walking the lobby with Elena Isabella on his shoulder. He was gently bouncing her, making a rhythmic shushing sound.

Aubrey looked into the infant's face. Her eyes were mere slits. Then they slowly closed. "She's out."

Daniel continued the soothing routine for another couple of minutes, walking from the vending machines to the potted palm tree in the corner. Aubrey's heart melted.

Daniel stopped the sound but continued walking. "Good. For such a tiny baby, she's got some serious volume."

"Well, her house is not exactly a quiet oasis."

He gently lowered himself onto the faux leather sofa. "Not to be nosy, but do you think you'll ever do this?" He cocked his head toward the sleeping baby.

Aubrey sat on a matching chair across from him. "Don't get me wrong. I love children, but I don't really want any of my own. How about you? You've already raised one. Would you do it all over again?"

"For a lot of years when Mac was younger, I thought I might. Now that I'm a young empty nester, I don't want anymore."

Ricardo and his seven-year-old son Caesar walked in.

"Aubrey! The Flying Cowboys are out there. Their planes are all in a row in front of the terminal. They signed my shirt!" The boy posed with his shirt showing off the front, then turned around and did the same with the back.

"Awesome!"

"They're waiting out the weather. If it doesn't clear up, they may be staying here tonight," Ricardo said.

"That will be great publicity for Skyways," Aubrey said.

Ricardo turned to Daniel. "Thank you. I'll take her now."

He secured his daughter in the carrier. "Come on. Let's go get Mom and Brother from T-ball practice."

Aubrey reached out a hand to Daniel. "Wanna come meet some YouTubers who make backcountry flying look easy?"

He smiled and took her hand.

Aubrey scanned the buffet table in the ballroom at the Arizona Biltmore. Abrazo Health always had their Christmas party at the iconic resort in the shadow of Camelback Mountain. Of course, the room was absolutely dazzling. The concave, stained glass skylight gave off a low hue while reflecting the electric holiday candles on the tables. She sighed. It might have been nice to have Daniel with her in all this modern opulence. Him being her plus-one at her mother's wedding was great. She looked over to the table where she was sitting with a few other nurses and technicians who had also come alone. *Let's not get too*

used to having him on your arm. After making some careful choices at the buffet and heading to her table, she locked eyes with Chad across the room. He held her gaze for a moment, then his eyes seemed to take in her form-fitting red dress. He looked away. *In your dreams, you son-of-a-bitch.*

Aubrey's evening with her colleagues had been wonderful. No shop talk, just catching up. Lisa hoped her baby would come before Christmas. Martin was taking his partner home to Barbados to meet his family. Sue was celebrating six months of sobriety. Now it was past time to get home to bed for her shift the next morning. Aubrey scanned the room; no sign of Chad.

She stepped into the parking garage carrying the gift basket she won. She'd share the wine, cheese, crackers, and other goodies with her mom and Charlie. Aubrey worked most holidays, but always planned a day to celebrate with her mom.

Seemingly out of nowhere, Chad appeared beside her. "Aubrey, let me walk you to your car."

"No, I'm fine."

He quickened his pace to keep up with her.

Chad positioned himself in front of her, turned, and stopped.

Aubrey stumbled on her heels, stopping to avoid running into him. She glared when he reached out a hand to steady her.

"You really don't want to talk?" He crossed his arms, pushing up his perfectly knotted red and green tie.

"What's there to talk about?"

"Look. Everything about what went down between us was wrong, and it was my fault."

"Well, I would have at least respected you if you had told me you had a beautiful wife and a growing family. But you wanted to cheat on them with me. I would have said no, but I would have respected you...Some, anyway."

He ran a hand over his clean-shaven chin. "I see that. When my beautiful family blew up in my face, my ex took the kids and moved back here. I sold my very successful practice and followed them. Crazy as it was, I had a fleeting thought that this new chapter might include you."

Her eyes narrowed.

He put up a hand. "I know. You would rightfully never trust me again. Also, I seriously didn't think you'd still be available."

Heat rose from her core to her chest. Her fist began to clench, but she relaxed it. "My relationship status is none of your business."

"No, it's not. But I hope you're with someone who deserves you."

"Good night, Chad."

He stepped aside, and she headed toward her car.

Aubrey's cell phone rang as she was leaving Banner University Medical Center.

"Aubrey, it's Sam. I've got a whole litter of puppies to bottle feed. Wanna come over and give me a hand?"

"Sure. It will take about a half hour."

"Perfect."

This would be a good night to find out where she really stood with Sam.

When Sam let her in, Aubrey could hear the whimper of newborn pups. He smiled, handed her a bottle, then led her to the hall bathroom.

"What's the story?"

She picked up one crying puppy at random, gently touching the pup's snout with the bottle's nipple. The newborn began sucking vigorously.

"They were found in some bushes. Their mother was a half a block away. Killed by a car." Sam put one pup back in the box, then picked up another.

She frowned. "That's too bad."

Once the litter of eight were fed and placed back in the newspaper and towel lined box, Aubrey and Sam went into the living room. Sam's arms encircled her waist and pulled her to him. His breath tickled the top of her ear.

"I've been thinking about you a lot lately." He bent down and kissed her full on the mouth.

Aubrey put her hand up and pulled away. "We can't tonight. It's the wrong time."

He nodded and stepped away, leaving more room between them. "You didn't mention that on the phone."

"You said you wanted help feeding puppies."

"I understand. My internet is down, so no streaming. Why don't you sit down? I'll make some popcorn."

She took a seat on Sam's sectional.

"Hey, how's that guy's dog doing?" Sam called from the kitchen.

"Great. Briscoe is 100%."

"Good." He brought the popcorn to the couch. "So, how've you been?"

"Great. My mom's wedding was really beautiful. They act like a couple of teenagers nowadays. Last week, I spotted signs of human trafficking on an ER patient. The young gal is now at the Streetlight Center."

He reached down to tie his shoe. "Good."

"How are things with you?"

He looked up as if he just realized she asked him a question. "Oh. Good. Same old. Same old at the shelter. My brother's coming to visit next month."

"Nice. I hope you two have a good time."

Silence.

"Sam?"

His eyes refocused on her. "Sorry. I've got a lot on my plate right now."

"I'm here to listen if you want talk about it."

He set the empty popcorn bowl on the coffee table. "It's nothing I want to go into right now."

Sam's phone chimed, and he picked it up checking a text.

"Everything okay?"

"Yeah, but I really do have to deal with this." He held up his phone. "You should go. I'll take care of the next feeding on my own."

He stood up and was halfway to the door before she even got up. She began to huff but squelched it.

"Okay." Aubrey caught up to him collecting her purse along the way.

He turned when he reached the door, but as soon as his eyes met hers, he looked past her shoulder then down.

What the fuck? Was the text from someone who wanted to have sex tonight?

She forced a smile. "I'll see you later."

"Yes." With stilted movements, Sam put his arms around her without pulling her close.

Once Aubrey reached her jeep, she jerked it into gear then took a deep slow breath before releasing the break.

Without sex or streaming, he can't even talk to me.

Aubrey raised her hangar door after the Events Committee meeting. The Christmas party potluck always required an extra meeting or two. She agreed to shop for the holiday themed plates and napkins on her next day off. After grabbing a beer from her fridge, she settled on her couch and took in the peace of the sunset hour.

Life had been anything but peaceful lately with her father's sporadic attempts to contact her and Chad's return to Arizona. Sam's recent attitude didn't help. Then there was the question of approaching Daniel about being an FWB. Wouldn't it alleviate some of the stress if she called her father to find out what he wanted? She pulled her cell phone out of her pocket and turned it over in her hand a few times.

The memory of Daniel and Mackenzie's phone call, where Mackenzie called her dad to help solve a problem, came back like it was happening right now. He was there when his daughter needed him. When Chad broke Aubrey's heart, she was estranged from both of her parents, so she had cried on Justine's shoulder. Statistically, if she had had a good relationship with her father, she never would have fallen for Chad in the first place.

He wasn't there when she needed him. Now, for some reason, he wanted to talk to her. Forget it. She put her phone back in her pocket and finished her beer.

Chapter Twelve

Daniel jotted a few notes in the Mooney's engine log, notating the completion of the repairs. A car approaching the open hangar caught his attention. He turned around to see Aubrey entering. Briscoe, tail wagging, ran up to her.

"Hi baby!" She scooped up the wriggling dog who licked her chin and cheeks. Then she turned toward Daniel. "You the only one here?"

"Yeah. I stayed to finish work on that Mooney over there." He motioned to the plane on his left. "Anything I can help you with?"

"Actually, my idle is too high. Can you adjust it? I can taxi over here."

He shrugged. "I'll just meet you at your hangar."

Daniel hastily retrieved his belongings from his locker, then brought down the door of the hangar and locked up.

He jumped into his truck and caught up to Aubrey's Challenger. After listening to the idle, he grabbed a few tools from the toolbox in the bed of his truck and made a few adjustments.

"Okay, fire it up again."

The engine purred.

While he put his tools away, Aubrey pushed her plane into her hangar.

"Anything else?" He turned, only to realize she was standing very close to him.

"Only this." She placed her lips on his and gently leaned into him, pushing him against his truck.

Daniel's heart seemed to skip a beat. In seconds, his hands found her waist and back, pulling her to him. The softness of her lips mingled with her rose and citrus perfume. Heat began to build in his core.

The sound of a car door closing caused another surge of adrenaline. He turned toward the sound, pushing Aubrey behind him, his hand at his right pocket.

"Aubrey?!"

A pilot Daniel had seen several times came around the front of the truck.

"Oh! I'm sorry! I need to talk to Aubrey." The man held both hands at chest level and took a step back.

Daniel relaxed. Aubrey came around out from behind him giving Daniel a quizzical, and annoyed look.

"I saw the light on in your hangar. My uncle is having chest pain. Please come take a look at him."

"Yes! Did you call 911?" Aubrey raced to her car.

"No, I hoped you could look at him first."

"Call them."

Daniel jumped into his truck and followed the pilot's car two rows north of Aubrey's hangar. If CPR were needed, two was always better than one.

Daniel stepped into the shower after adjusting the temperature.

Fortunately, the man with chest pain had a normal heart rhythm when tested by the paramedics' equipment. Still, he opted to go to the

ER as a precaution. The pilot, Rick, didn't seem bothered by Daniel's initial defensive posture once his uncle was being attended to. Would his high alert ever go away? It was better than when he first left the force, but on some level, it would remain his constant companion.

The scents of Skyways Aviation seemed to slide off his body and down the drain. The real scent he wanted to hold onto was in his memory. The scent of Aubrey's skin, hair, and perfume. He had been told by her and others that she didn't want a relationship. No, he had been told she didn't commit. At any rate, he had been told to be careful. That kiss satisfied, but also left him hungry. But what did it mean to her?

Aubrey had just landed the Bonanza after an afternoon of practicing power-off landings. As soon as she pushed her plane back into the hangar, her phone chimed.

> *My place at 5:00 or after you get off work? I'm off early today. I'll make pizza.*

She sighed. It was Sam. The whole point of a friends-with-benefits relationship was that there was a friendship involved. Last time they had sex, it felt more like a hookup. The time after that, they couldn't have sex and he tried to show it didn't matter, but it obviously did. It was time. She texted back.

> *I'm off today. Let's meet at Paseo Highlands Park. Send me your Dutch Bros. order.*

With a cinnamon latte in one hand and a caramel iced coffee in the other, Aubrey swung her hip to close the Challenger's door. In a second, Sam was beside her.

"Here," Sam said, taking a drink out of her hands. "I'll carry my drink. Thank you, by the way."

He had changed out of his scrubs and wore a new pair of jeans and a red Arizona Cardinals sweatshirt.

They made their way to a park bench across from the playground, near the tennis courts.

Sam took a sip from his latte, then turned toward Aubrey. "Instead of pizza at my place, we're doing Dutch Bros. at the park. I think I know what this is about."

Aubrey nodded. "You're a good guy, Sam, and I'll always be your friend. But I need a break from the benefits between us."

"I understand. I knew when I went over to help Daniel with Briscoe that our time together was short."

Aubrey gave him a quizzical look. "I am cultivating a FWB relationship with him, not an exclusive relationship."

"Not yet, anyway. Obviously, there was the stress of the situation, but there was an undercurrent between you two. I know once Briscoe was stabilized, he was trying to figure out what I was to you. Honestly, I was doing the same."

Aubrey shrugged.

"Look Aubrey, we've known each other a long time. I don't think you would turn loose of us unless you thought there was something better ahead."

A start coursed through her. Humble was not a word she would use to describe Sam.

Daniel pulled up to Aubrey's hangar after he had finished work. She texted him an hour ago saying they needed to talk.

When he pulled up, she moved from her cluttered desk to the small table and chairs that butted up against the metal wall.

"Hey, have a seat."

Once again, her smile lit up the small space. He took the chair she motioned to.

Aubrey took a deep breath and looked down at the table before meeting his eyes. "I made a mistake the other night."

Daniel chuckled. "Well, if it's what I'm thinking it is, it was an awfully nice mistake. Feel free to make it again."

She laughed for a second and rolled her eyes. "Kissing you was not the mistake. It was kissing you without all the cards on the table."

He looked down at the table between them and motioned across it.

"Okay. I don't do relationships in the traditional sense. I do friends with benefits or FWBs. I have enjoyed getting to know you these last few months. I'm definitely attracted to you, and if you're open to it, I'd like to explore an FWB relationship with you."

For a moment, it was like cold water splashed in his face. Aubrey looked away, sitting a little stiffer and more upright. He looked down and scratched the back of his neck, gaining control of his facial expression.

"Correct me if I'm wrong. This means we would have a sexual relationship, but you wouldn't be my girlfriend."

Her posture relaxed a little, and she turned back to him "Yes."

"You currently have relations with others, and I would be free to do the same."

"That's right."

Heat started to build, radiating to his chest and groin. That kiss opened the floodgates he'd been pushing against for months. Now an invitation.

Think, Daniel, think.

"I want to think about it before I decide if this is for me."

When Daniel drove off, Aubrey pulled her plane out of the hangar. She then grabbed her broom from the corner and began sweeping. She usually used the blower. Today it was the push broom.

Too much for one day. Breaking up with Sam was not a decision she took lightly. Then to turn right around and invite Daniel into her FWB circle. She should have given it a day or two, but the spur-of-the-moment kiss rushed her decision. Their conversation didn't go as well as she had hoped, but then it didn't go as poorly as it could have. Tears stung her eyes as she replayed some of the slut-shaming reactions a few men had had throughout the years. Maybe Daniel didn't accept it right away, but he was at least respectful. He wanted to think about it. No problem. Judging from his reaction, FWB was new to him. What did she think he would do, close her hangar door and take her then and there?

Another wave of sadness. He may very well reject her offer, but she likely wouldn't be slut-shamed this time.

Daniel walked with Briscoe down the now-familiar path to the complex's large dog park. He zipped his windbreaker against the cooling evening. When he left Aubrey two nights ago, he said he wanted to think over her invitation to be friends with benefits. That was after overriding thoughts of then and there inviting her to his place.

His neighbor Rochelle came walking toward him from the dog park.

She waved. "Thank you again for taking Rufus out when I got stuck at work last week."

"Anytime."

Her print dress clung and fell in all the right places. Thirtyish, attractive, divorced. He considered Rochelle a possibility since they met back in September. He figured he might pursue her, if she was still available when he was ready.

Daniel reached the dog park and began throwing a ball for Briscoe.

His attraction to Aubrey was undeniable, but he always pushed it away since he had concerns and didn't want to be tied down. Now things made sense. She didn't want an exclusive relationship as he had now heard straight from her. In addition to Rochelle, there was Sonja. She had made it known that she was attracted to him. Could he really enjoy Aubrey and be unattached? What was causing him to hesitate? Was it just that an FWB relationship was a foreign concept to him, or was it the thought of sharing? Years ago, he broke off a relationship when he found out his girlfriend was seeing other men. With Aubrey, he would know he wasn't the only one. He cringed. Did he want to see other women along with Aubrey? He couldn't keep her waiting for an answer too long.

Aubrey parked her car across from the pool at Deer Valley Park and headed for the dog park. The Saturday afternoon traffic on 19th Avenue whizzed by. After four days of being incommunicado, Daniel had texted and asked her to meet him there. Now she had some idea of how Sam must have felt meeting her at Paseo Highlands.

There he was on the same bench as a few months ago. He smiled when she sat down beside him, but the smile did not reach his eyes. Briscoe ran up to her. She picked him up, and he licked her chin.

"Okay. That's enough!" She set him down, and he ran off across the grass toward some other dogs.

When she turned her attention back to Daniel, he took a deep breath. *Here it comes.*

"I've been thinking a lot about our conversation at your hangar."

"Okay."

"The fact that I'm attracted to you is not in question. I'm just not comfortable being one of the guys."

Her heart squeezed in her chest. She looked down momentarily, then back to his face.

He continued. "I don't want a relationship right now, but I want there to be one if I'm going to give my all to a woman again."

She grabbed his hand. "I understand. FWB is not for everyone."

His shoulders lowered, and his face relaxed. He squeezed her hand. "Friends?"

Aubrey smiled. "Absolutely."

Chapter Thirteen

Aubrey arrived early at Skyways and let herself in. After two trips to her car carrying in bags of food, she started the coffee in the break room. Then she laid out an assortment of bagels, donuts, and muffins on the counter. Every year for Nate's birthday, Justine asked Aubrey to pick up the breakfast items and decorate the table in the breakroom. Aubrey always made sure the decorations were birthday themed, not Christmas, as Nate often expressed chagrin at being born in December.

Daniel was the first to arrive that morning looking fresh from a full night's sleep. Her heart squeezed for a moment, then relaxed.

He glanced at the table. "Looks great."

Aubrey looked up from laying out napkins and saw Daniel reach into his front pocket and place a firearm in his locker. "Whoa. You carry a gun?"

"Yeah, Arizona and Montana have reciprocity, so I didn't have to reapply for my Concealed Carry Permit."

"I know you would have carried on Highway Patrol; I just didn't know you still did. I've never been particularly comfortable with guns."

"I didn't think anything made you uncomfortable."

"Guns do."

Daniel tilted his head. "Why?"

"First off, in the ER, I've seen what they can do. But even before I became a nurse, I never liked them. My father always had one at home, but he demanded that I never touch it."

"He should have taught you how to handle one instead. I learned from an early age how to shoot and safely handle a firearm. Mackenzie was nine when Jen and I started teaching her."

Aubrey shuddered.

"My point is, knowing how to handle a gun properly takes away the fear, but not the respect or responsibility."

The break room door opened behind her.

Aubrey turned toward Nate and Justine. They all blurted out. "Happy birthday!"

Daniel was washing parts in the industrial sink while replaying that morning's conversation with Aubrey. A car pulled up and stopped outside the hangar. He looked toward Nate's office. Nate was on the phone. The others were either at lunch or off on parts runs. Daniel set down the parts and headed to the vehicle.

A man in his sixties, wearing a gray tailored suit and blue-patterned silk tie, stepped out of a Cadillac Escalade. He looked around for a moment.

Daniel approached. "Can I help you?"

"Yes." He looked toward Nate's office. "I need to talk to Nate, but I see he's busy at the moment."

The blue eyes that held his for a moment had an intensity behind them.

"Would you like to wait in the lobby?"

"No, but thank you. I'll just wait here."

"Okay. Can I get you a bottled water?"

Nate appeared behind Daniel, putting a hand on his shoulder. "Thanks Dan." Nate turned toward the expensively dressed man. "Hey there, Franklin. Nice to see you."

Daniel went back to the sink. The conversation was none of his business. Still, he turned the faucet on lower than he had it before.

"Aubrey's not here, is she?"

"No, but she said you've been trying to reach her. Now you need to back off and give her time."

He sighed. "For all the good it will do, tell her I really need to talk to her."

Realization washed over Daniel. Everything about this man's commanding presence backed up Aubrey's description of him. His demeanor, though, not exactly what he expected. Then again, Daniel was a stranger, and Franklin had a goal to accomplish so he wouldn't have been condescending toward Daniel.

"I'll tell her."

He sighed again. "Thank you, Nate. Truly."

Daniel glanced behind him. Franklin's shoulders were just a little lower than when he arrived. Defeat that he wouldn't let show. The power struggles between teenage Aubrey and her father must have been amazing. Aubrey clearly fought back and seemed to be getting the best of him, but how many times in her life had she lost against him?

Aubrey was waiting on a porch swing in her alcove when Daniel's truck pulled up. She kept thinking about Daniel's words indicating that nothing seemed to make her uncomfortable. Of course, that wasn't true. They both knew no one was completely fearless. A few days after their conversation, she called him and said she would give him a chance to teach her the basics of shooting.

"So where are we going?"

"C2 Tactical in Scottsdale. It should be pretty quiet at this hour on a weekday."

She took a deep breath. "Good, I don't want to be surrounded by blasts and vibration."

"There will be some of that, but it should be at a minimum. By the way, what made you decide you wanted to do this?"

"Realizing my fear was not based on experience. After today, I may decide I'm okay with guns or I may decide I still don't like them."

"Fair enough."

When they arrived, Daniel collected his pistol case, earphones, and safety glasses. "We'll have to rent your ear and eye protection. I only have one set."

She gave him a coy smile. "You do this right, and I may wind up buying my own."

He returned her smile "Challenge accepted."

They entered the store which was brightly lit from the sun through the front windows and the LED lights in the ceiling. Several locked, plexiglass cases showcased guns for sale. Gun cases and other supplemental items were displayed throughout the store. Adorning the walls were videos of people shooting, along with posters containing slogans of safety and preparedness. Many depicted women. The employees in their black, collared pullovers each had a firearm strapped to their side.

She leaned over to Daniel. "Bet this place doesn't get robbed."

He chuckled and put an arm around her. She relaxed against him.

While Aubrey read and initialed the long list of rules and precautions, Daniel chatted with a petite, Hispanic woman he referred to as Sonja. She was nearing forty, and clearly took care of herself. He asked if it was possible to get a lane in a room to themselves. Aubrey heard her say lanes 1-6 were currently empty, but she couldn't guarantee they would stay that way.

When Aubrey looked up from the tablet, Sonja was leaning toward Daniel looking him in the eyes. Is this woman why Daniel turned down her FWB offer? She huffed quietly. FWB is not for everybody. He had a right to live his life as he chose, just like she did. She read and signed the last two precautions.

Sonja handed Aubrey her ear and eye protection with a smile that was professional not warm.

With a hand on her back, Daniel guided Aubrey toward the automatic door which opened with a whisper. Once in the antechamber, they waited for the door to close.

"This way." He motioned to their left, and pushed the button letting them into a concrete room with twelve lanes, six in each sectioned-off area. Both sections were empty.

He led her to lane one. Each lane was separated by plexiglass and black metal octagons bordered in electric blue. Daniel taped a target containing five small targets to a piece of cardboard held by a clip before hitting the button to send it five yards away. He then unpacked his gun case on the counter at the front of the lane.

She watched closely while he put ammunition into the magazine of his 9-millimeter Smith and Wesson. He pushed the magazine into the handle of the gun and racked it. He explained every step as to how and why he did what he did.

"Always keep the firearm pointed down range. Treat all guns like they are loaded, even if you know for sure they are not."

"No problem there."

"Okay, take the grip in both of your hands." He guided her hands around the grip, positioning them in the correct shooting hold.

She took in the scent of citrus and bergamot on his skin.

He moved behind her. "You need the correct stance to shoot accurately and deal with the recoil. Your feet are too close together."

She moved her feet further apart. He put one foot between hers.

"A little more." He nudged each foot an inch or two farther apart.

"Put the red dot of the site between the two white dots. Once they are lined up, put the three dots where you want the bullet to hit on the target."

He stayed close behind her. "When you are ready, slowly squeeze the trigger."

She took a deep breath, then gently pulled the trigger. A loud bang rang through the chamber while powerful vibration ran up her arms in a wave. Once she caught her breath, she laughed.

Daniel smiled down at her. "Good. Low and to the left, but you hit within the target. Take your time and try again."

This time, she anticipated the recoil knowing how it felt. The bullet hit outside of the target. She aimed again and emptied the fifteen-round magazine.

Aubrey slid into the pink half booth, half table at The Sugar Bowl. The muffled sound of gunfire, the vibration down her arms, Daniel's scent and touch all melded together creating heat within her core.

Sonja? What was she to Daniel? Did he share the attraction? He could be hard to read at times. If he was attracted to her, he wasn't showing it.

"You did great in there." Daniel took the chair opposite her.

"Thanks. I had a good teacher. That's why I have brand new ear and eye protection."

After perusing the menu and ordering, Aubrey noticed Daniel's face take on a more serious appearance. He looked around at the splash of pink and white surrounding them, then seemed to study the huge impressionist style painting on the wall beside him.

"This place been here long?"

"Very. It's a fixture of Old Town Scottsdale. My parents used to take me here for birthdays and other occasions when I was young. It was a compromise. I wanted to have birthday parties at Mc Donald's where some of my friends had theirs. My dad wanted to take me to nice restaurants instead. My mother came up with The Sugar Bowl. It wasn't fast food, but it was a fun place where I could invite all of my friends."

"I think we all want the best for our children."

Aubrey's heart twisted at the memory of her father's lecture requiring her to stop spending time with a boy. She was only thirteen at the time, but she had fallen hard for him. The boy's family were local bikers and not up to Franklin's standards.

"Maybe. I thought it was great until I got old enough to figure out that all the name-brand clothes and expensive toys were all for his image rather than for me."

"All?"

"It certainly seemed that way. The big reason he let me take flying lessons was that a pilot's license looked great on a college application."

Their plates arrived, and they took a moment to savor the burgers and malts.

"You were right about this place. The food's excellent."

"I know where to eat around here."

"Speaking of your father. He came by Skyways a couple days ago."

"That's what Nate said. Apparently, he really wants to talk to me. I don't know what he hopes to accomplish. He basically told me that if I was going to live my own life, I was going to do it without him and his money. Now, out of nowhere, he wants to contact me."

"Aren't you curious what he wants? If you hear what he has to say, it doesn't mean anything has to change."

"I just don't see a reason to talk to him." She took a long sip of her chocolate malt to cool the heat rising to her neck and face.

"I wouldn't mind being with you if you decide to meet with him."

She slammed down her malt glass. "I can handle him by myself. I'm not afraid of him."

Daniel put his hands up in a surrender motion. "Okay. I was offering moral support, not protection."

"Why do you care whether I talk to him or not?"

"It just might be beneficial for you. Also, I know how I would feel if my daughter didn't see or talk to me."

"You're nothing like him. You didn't plan her whole life out and expect her to fit into your neat little package with no regard for who she is and what she wants."

A family at another table turned to look in their direction. Aubrey took another long sip of her malt.

"No, I didn't," he said quietly.

The server brought the check and cleared away their plates. Aubrey snatched up the check and put down her credit card.

"I can get the check."

"No, you paid for the shooting. I got dinner."

His hands raised in defeat.

The silence on the drive home was a wall between them. While being yelled at or cursed at put him on high alert, total silence wasn't any better. When someone was belligerent, there were ways to diffuse the situation. With silence, you didn't know what someone was thinking or what they were going to do next. *It's Aubrey, everything's fine.* His heart rate slowed, and his shoulders relaxed.

"I'm sorry. There's a lot I don't seem to understand about your relationship with your father. I clearly said something I shouldn't have. I didn't mean to upset you." He stopped the truck in front of Aubrey's house.

"I know." She squeezed his hand and looked into his eyes.

She opened the truck's back door and took out her newly purchased shooting gear. When the door closed with a quiet thud, Aubrey did not look back.

Aubrey awoke at five o'clock in the evening after coming home from her shift that ended at seven that morning. She hadn't been to the airport since her argument with Daniel a few days ago. Her words to him rang in her head. She said he was nothing like her father, and he wasn't. He wasn't the first person to recommend she contact her father, and he wouldn't be the last.

She threw back the covers and got up to get ready for tonight's shift. If she cut a few corners, she might be able to catch Daniel leaving work.

Daniel called Briscoe from his corner and headed through the lobby to the parking lot. He smiled and picked up his pace when he saw Aubrey's Challenger pull into a parking space next to his truck.

She got out right as he reached their vehicles, looking beautiful in scrubs and a ponytail.

Briscoe ran to her. Aubrey picked up the little dog, cuddling him.

"Hey." She glanced at Daniel for a second.

"Hi. I've been wondering how you were doing since the other night."

"I'm fine. I'm sorry. I know you meant well." She handed him his dog.

He nodded. "I did. But in my law enforcement career, I've seen all kinds of family dynamics." He ran a hand through his hair. "You know whether or not you should contact him. I shouldn't have tried to steer you in that direction."

"It's fine. I'm not going to tell you not to share your opinion - even if your opinion pisses me off."

He chuckled.

She looked down at her phone. "I'm doing a night shift up the street, so I've got to go."

After an awkward hug, she got into her car. He stared after her departing vehicle. She was so strong yet so vulnerable.

Chapter Fourteen

On his way to the breakroom, Daniel took off his Skyways windbreaker.

"Heading to lunch?" Nate was coming out of his office putting on his jacket.

"Yeah, do I need to do something first?"

"No, we're all heading to the Christmas party in hangar 16-8. It's a great potluck. I figured you were coming with us?"

"Oh. I forgot about the party, so I don't have anything to bring."

"No worries, I'm bringing a huge sub that counts for all of us."

Daniel put his windbreaker back on. In moments, Nate returned from the breakroom with the sandwich, and everyone piled into Nate and Justine's Suburban.

When they arrived, several pilots, mechanics, and airport administrators along with their significant others stood around various tables dishing up food. Cold, hot, sweet, savory, there was something for every palate. Children of a wide range of ages ate and ran around.

Daniel had just dished up a paper plate with several of the offerings when he turned and saw Aubrey coming toward the table with a crockpot full of something that smelled mildly spicy.

She beamed at Daniel as she set the crockpot down. "You have to try my chili. It's probably different from what they make in Montana. Mine is very Southwestern."

He set down his plate and grabbed a bowl, into which she ladled some chili. Daniel, with a bowl of chili in one hand and a plate in the other, found Nate who had saved a seat for him at one of the fold-out tables. The light breeze mixed with warm sun was reminiscent of an early fall day in Great Falls.

Aubrey flitted around talking to several people. Children and teens ran up and hugged her. As usual, she seemed to know everyone. She approached two pilots he had seen around. Was one of them a "friend?" A few minutes later, the trio separated, and the two men joined two women who appeared to be significant others. Probably not FWBs then.

"Dan?" Nate nudged his arm. "I was just saying it should be fine for you to take a couple days off around New Years for Mackenzie's visit."

"Oh, sorry. I'm so full that I'm zoning. That's great. I would love to spend some extra time with Mackenzie. Thank you."

"You know. Right now, I'm probably the only one noticing that you're watching Aubrey's every move."

Daniel rose from his chair. "Got it. I think I'll go mingle."

He looked around and found some A and Ps from AreoGuard and joined their conversation.

What Aubrey chose to do with her life was not his concern. They were friends, that's all. But why did she have to look so damn good in form-fitting jeans and a light blue sweater sprinkled with snowflakes?

As the party was settling down, Daniel rejoined Nate. Out of nowhere, a Nerf ball landed on the table in front of them, upsetting empty plates and soda cans. Daniel moved into a defensive position, then relaxed.

A girl approached the table sheepishly. "Sorry."

Nate grabbed the ball. "No problem, Katrina. Go long!"

The preteen giggled and ran several feet from the tables. Then Nate threw her the ball.

"Well. Good company. Good food, but time to get back to it," Nate said.

Daniel headed for the SUV along with the others.

In his peripheral, vision he caught sight of Aubrey's sweater. She was approaching him.

"What time do you think you'll finish up tonight?"

"Not sure. Why?"

"This is the perfect time of year for a sunset flight. It would be a great way to really see your new home state."

He looked into her beaming face. "Why don't I see you at your hangar at 5:00?"

Daniel swiped his pass at the entrance to the north hangars. Initially he was going to leave Skyways and go straight to Aubrey's hangar. However, a moment of distraction caused aviation fuel to douse the front of his shirt. Knowing he would be in close quarters with Aubrey, he left a half hour early to shower and change. Aubrey was waiting for him when he arrived. An olive drab T-shirt under a soft pink fleece had replaced the snowflake sweater she wore earlier.

"Sorry I'm a little late."

"You're not. In fact, I just finished the preflight."

He climbed up the wing after she entered the cockpit. Once he was belted in and shut the door, the light scent of lotion and citrusy body wash emanated from her. Her eyes darted from the pre-take-off checklist to the gages while she flipped switches and pulled back on the yoke, turning it right, then left, brows knit together in concentration.

She turned to him beaming and started the engine. A mild surge coursed through him.

After the run up and clearance from the tower, the plane seemed to glide into the air. The cool, cloudless evening lent itself to a smooth flight. Daniel looked out the windshield and side windows as Arizona's rugged landscape spread out before them like a brown and green blanket. Clusters of neighborhoods, some with golf courses, some without, interrupted the continuous desert. Near the neighborhoods were areas of ranches and mansions on large parcels of land.

"We're over Cave Creek and Carefree where I grew up." Aubrey motioned toward the windshield.

She continued flying east then banked the plane to the south. The sunset exploded off to their right. Taller, sharper mountains took the place of the small hills that punctuated the area they had just flown over. Sections of green trees gave way to areas of burned trees along the slopes of the mountains. The vertical faces were bare, with neutral shades of the lightest tan to brown and nearly red.

Aubrey taught him the names of the various lakes and pointed out the Salt River which connected several of them. Dry stream beds seemed to connect the lakes as well.

Daniel was familiar with the Four Peaks Mountain range. He had seen the mountains off in the distance several times going to the East Valley on parts runs or for ball games. Close up from a plane, the peaks looked like four sections of boulders piled together.

She pointed out a little strip of land in the mountains near Canyon Lake. "That's Tortilla Flats. One of the last stagecoach stops along the Apache Trail. You should take your bike there when you get fully comfortable with curvy roads."

After banking the plane west and north, turning back, the system of canals snaked through neighborhoods and agricultural areas. Soon he recognized the Loop 101 Freeway and the small hills leading back to Deer Valley Airport.

After a beautiful landing, they taxied back to her hangar the blue trail of lights framing the path.

Aubrey studied Daniel's back and shoulders when he exited the plane, heat radiating from her core.

He helped her push the plane back in the hangar, and she took a moment at her desk to record the flight in her Pilot's Logbook. Warmth flooded her knowing his eyes were upon her.

She stood up and held his gaze. His eyes told her she was already naked on her couch. "Are you sure about this?"

"Nope. I think this may be a bad idea."

She walked past him, then turned to him as she hit the button closing the hangar door. The door settled into its place with a light clang.

"How bad?"

He closed the distance between them in quick strides.

"Terrible." He put his hands around her waist, then to her back, pulling her to him. "But I don't care."

His lips found hers with his tongue brushing them gentle but insistent. Her breathing quickened as her lips parted allowing him entry. A wave like an electric current traveled from her mouth down her throat through her breasts to where her legs joined. She tightened her arms around him, feeling him hard against her abdomen. *Please don't let this be a dream. Or if it is, please don't wake me now.*

She pulled away long enough to slide her hands under his sweater, guiding it over his head and tossing it on her desk.

His lips again found hers as he slowly unzipped her fleece. She drew in her breath as his hands brushed over her nipples before sliding the jacket off her shoulders and down her arms.

He threw the fleece onto her desk chair, then she grabbed his hand and urgently led him around her airplane.

"Careful." She said, ducking under the tail. She turned toward him. His nostrils flared, and his gaze darkened. She slowly removed her T-shirt and reclined onto the couch. *Come get me. I'm all yours.*

He yanked off his own T-shirt and threw it somewhere behind him. Easing himself onto her, the deliciousness of his weight settled upon her. He sucked in her lower lip before his tongue slowly entered her again. More electricity coursed through her in unbearable surges.

She pushed just slightly against his chest. "I need you inside me!"

He seemed to drink her in, then gave a mischievous smile. "All in good time."

His hands reached around her back lifting her slightly, undoing the hook, freeing her tingling breasts from her bra. She threw it somewhere in the direction of Daniel's shirt. Now his lips and tongue created a trail of fire down her neck, stopping to give her another grin before he took a hard nipple into his mouth. A moan escaped her lips, but she squelched it knowing she could be heard through the vent. While one nipple stood perfectly erect as his tongue glided over it, the other was being rolled, kneaded, and caressed sending waves straight to her core. Her moans were now whispers against the top of his head.

He raised up and straddled her. "I noticed you quieted down. Maybe I need to up my game."

His hands ran down her ribcage and waist. She squirmed at the slight tickle. He ran his fingers just inside the waistband of her jeans before unfastening them. She ached for him as he eased her jeans down her thighs seemingly inch by inch. Once she was only in panties, his lips were again on hers, hands in her hair, giving a slight tug. His erection pressed against her was absolute nirvana.

She could barely speak but managed to utter, "Now," before jerking both jeans and briefs down his thighs. She then reached for her panties.

He gently took her hands. "Let me do that," he said in a raspy whisper.

She moved her hands away, taking in his now naked form, while he guided her panties down her legs much quicker than he did her jeans. She reached into her purse on the arm of the couch, pulling out a condom and tearing off the wrapper. He drew in his breath, his gaze fiery as she unrolled it over him.

She lay back and relaxed while he eased himself into her. Her breath caught. In a few seconds, she took in the full length of him. Rhythmic thrusts in and against her brought her closer and closer to the edge until she gave a muffled cry. Several waves coursed through her as she grabbed and released him until, exhausted, she relaxed beneath him. With the strength she had left, she tightened around him. His face contorted in ecstasy when he gave one final hard thrust and collapsed with his head beside hers. She held him and stroked his back, taking in his scent.

Sleep will come easy tonight. Aubrey threw her clothes into the hamper, then set her pajamas on the shower chair she kept outside her walk-in shower.

The warm water coursed down her body, as she relived the feel of Daniel's hands and lips on her skin. Daniel was an FWB now, and a damn good one at that. Of course, she was disappointed when he initially turned her down, but it wasn't until his amber eyes burned with passion that she realized how much she had been wanting him.

She had thought of inviting him to her place afterward, figuring the drive would revive him and they would go for round two. But then Daniel didn't know the rule about not sleeping over, and that wasn't the time to tell him.

She closed her eyes and stood a little longer under the cascading water.

Halfway between sleeping and waking, visions of Aubrey in her hangar played through Daniel's memory. Did last night really happen, or was it just an incredible dream? He slowly opened his eyes while reaching for the other side of his bed. Empty. For a fleeting moment, it felt like Aubrey would be there, warm and bare breasted beside him. He huffed and turned over onto his back.

The crate between the closet and bathroom began to rattle. When Daniel swung his legs over the side of the bed, Briscoe began turning several circles.

"Okay. Walk and breakfast," he said opening the door.

Briscoe burst from the crate and began doing zoomies around the room while Daniel threw on some clothes. He laughed as his heart swelled.

The previous night returned as he laced up his shoes. It had been real, for sure. The warmth of her skin against his hands and lips. The look in her eyes as she relaxed her knees, allowing him entrance into the deepest part of her. Her muffled cries when he brought her closer and closer to the peak, then carried her over it. She had been completely his...For that night, anyway.

A cold breeze hit him in the face when he opened his door. Damn it. She wasn't just his. She was his and how many others'? He woke up ready for an encore. Maybe she did too. If she did, who would she choose?

His phone chimed Aubrey's Daybreak ringtone.

"Hey. How'd you sleep?"

Chapter Fifteen

D aniel parked his truck next to the Kawasaki in the airport parking lot and went around to the back to get his toolbox.

Mackenzie got out the passenger side and looked over the bike. "Nice."

"Thanks. I enjoy it when the battery's not giving me trouble." He removed the gas tank to gain access to the battery.

Mackenzie had flown in the day before New Year's Eve after spending Christmas with Jen and Wyatt and Daniel's relatives. Daniel spent Christmas Eve with Nate and Justine and Christmas with Ray and Vanessa. While Aubrey worked all of the holidays, there was some "celebrating" with her throughout the season. However, she made herself scarce when Mac flew in.

"Okay, that should be it." Daniel stood up and turned the key.

The sport bike purred to life. "Follow me home in the truck."

"How about you take me for a spin on it first?"

Daniel's eyes met hers. "You realize that if something happened to you on that bike, your mother would have my head? Forget about hiring it done. She would come down here and do it herself."

"Nothing is going to happen to her on the bike with you driving."

Daniel and Mackenzie turned at the sound of Aubrey's voice behind them. The sun, low in the sky, mixing with her blonde hair created an aura.

"Where'd you come from?" Daniel smiled.

"I was leaving an Events' Committee meeting and saw your truck. Thought I'd stop by." Aubrey approached Mackenzie with her hand extended. "You must be Mackenzie. Daniel talks about you all the time. I'm Aubrey."

Mackenzie took her hand. "Yes, he's talked about you too."

"Come on, Daniel take her for a spin around the airport. You won't let anything happen to her. I'll get Ray's spare helmet out of the hangar."

Daniel sighed. "Hop on."

When Aubrey handed her the helmet, Mackenzie giggled and got on the bike.

After cruising around the airport without incident, the father and daughter returned to the parking lot outside Skyways. Mackenzie dismounted the bike, pulled off the borrowed helmet, and let out a whoop of joy.

Daniel took off his own helmet and pointed a finger at Mackenzie. "Now don't you start thinking about getting one. The car your mom and I got you is fine for Colorado."

Her lips turned up in a smirk. "I know. I'll just ride your bike when I visit you here."

Aubrey laughed.

Daniel turned to Aubrey. "If she gets a bike anytime in the next ten years, I'm holding you personally responsible."

"Dad and I are going to ... Where are we going?"

"Manuel's."

"Yes. Would you like to come with us, Aubrey?"

Aubrey looked to Daniel, who nodded.

Manuel's was warm compared to the outside where the temperature had dropped quickly since sunset. Aubrey was seated in a booth where she waited for Daniel and Mackenzie to finish dropping off the Kawasaki at Daniel's place.

Once they arrived, they took off their jackets and slid into the booth across from Aubrey. Mackenzie appeared to take in the plants and parrot sculptures that decorated the upper alcoves.

"This place been here long?" Mackenzie asked after glancing at the white wall fountain near the entrance to the kitchen doors.

"Very. It's family owned, but the original couple are gone now." Aubrey spooned salsa onto her small, vermillion plate.

"I like supporting family owned and small businesses rather than chains." Mackenzie spooned both the hot sauce and salsa onto her plate, sampling both.

"So, Mackenzie, what is your major?"

"Outdoor Recreation Economy. The degree covers a wide variety of positions in state and national parks.

"She likes to work outdoors like I do."

Mackenzie nodded. Looking up at her dad, she smiled at him. "I'll be able to get a job anywhere."

"Yeah, like…. Arizona." Daniel nudged her.

"Or Hawaii, Utah, Colorado, or back home in Montana, to name a few."

Daniel chuckled. "You'll know where you want to go when the time comes."

The server took their order, and the busser returned with a new chip bowl.

Mackenzie's expressions were so much like Daniel's when she talked and listened. They had the same honey hair but different eyes.

"This salsa is very good." Mackenzie spooned more salsa onto her plate, leaving the hot sauce alone.

Daniel dipped a chip and took a small bite. "It's too hot for me tonight. Sometimes I can handle it, but not tonight."

"My friend Kristen is from Texas. We started going to farmer's markets on weekends. Several of us pool our money. She buys the ingredients and makes the best homemade salsa."

When the food arrived, Mackenzie seemed to switch gears. "So, Dad says you're a nurse."

"Yes, 10 years now."

"Had you always wanted to be one or did you stumble across it?"

"When I was in junior high, I used to get pretty bad headaches. My school nurse was so kind in helping me deal with them. I told my parents I wanted to be a nurse just like her. My father told me I was free to get my nursing degree after I got my business finance degree. That way, I could pay for nursing school myself."

"Oh. I'm sorry to hear that." Mackenzie's eyes flashed as she turned to Daniel. "You never said stuff like that."

Daniel shook his head. "No, but when you were nine, I did say you weren't allowed to juggle knives."

She rolled her eyes and nudged Daniel.

Daniel turned back to Aubrey. "You still became a nurse, so what happened?"

"A few years later, when I was 15, my friend's little brother seriously wrecked his bike right in front of us. I jumped into action. When the paramedics arrived, they asked who had attended to him. They complimented my work. It was then that I knew nursing was my calling."

Mackenzie had pushed her empty plate away and was leaning forward on her elbows. "And your father?"

"I kept it from him and got my degree after I left home."

"Good for you!" Mackenzie said with a fire behind her eyes.

Once outside, Aubrey and Mackenzie squeezed hands before Mackenzie headed to the truck. Aubrey then hugged Daniel.

"Good job, Dad." She whispered.

The next night, Daniel took Mackenzie to Arrowhead Mall for dinner and to shop for some things she needed. Now that the holidays were over, the mall with its second-floor food court was quiet on this weekday evening. After ordering from Panda Express, he found a table. Moments later, Mackenzie came over with her tray from Panera.

As Daniel settled into his teriyaki chicken, he noticed Mackenzie bite her lower lip while glancing at the ceiling. "What's on your mind?"

She looked down for a moment, then into his face. "It was nice having dinner with Aubrey last night, and I like her."

"But?"

"I'm picking up on some things. Like I think she has issues with how her father was when she was growing up."

"She does."

"Okay. Be careful. I know some girls who have daddy issues, and they make lousy girlfriends. I just don't want you to get hurt."

He squeezed her hand. "I appreciate that. I'll take care of myself. You just make sure you stay safe on campus."

"I will. I'm doing everything you told me to do."

"Which is?"

She rattled off the safety precautions he taught her. He fist-bumped his daughter when she finished the list. On the way out to parking lot, Daniel's mood darkened. Mackenzie's warning played on a loop. Technically though, Aubrey wasn't a girlfriend. Not really, anyway.

Chapter Sixteen

After waking up from a Monday night shift to a free Tuesday afternoon, Aubrey ate a leisurely meal on her back patio. The winter grass of her back yard was a brilliant green. A text from Nate told her that the BAS shoulder harness kit she had him order had arrived, and that Daniel would be starting on them today.

After putting on some jeans, her cowboy boots, and a long-sleeved aqua blue T-shirt, she headed for Skyways.

When she arrived, Nate was just backing out of his parking space. She entered the surprisingly quiet hangar to find Daniel in the back seat of her plane. The headliner was down, his arms and eyes toward the ceiling while he installed the mounting bracket. The front passenger seat was pushed to where the backrest touched the dash.

"Where is everybody?" Aubrey hoisted herself up onto the plane's wing.

"Slow day. I think Nate just left for an errand. Everyone else left for the day. I wanted to at least get the first shoulder harness in before I head home."

Aubrey scooted up on the wing to where she leaned into the doorway with her back rested against the folded front seat. She studied Daniel's slight frown and laser focused eyes as he cut a hole in the headliner where the harness would come through.

He set down his cutting tool still looking at the ceiling. "Can I ask you a personal question?"

"You can ask me anything you want. Whether or not I answer is up to me."

Daniel shook his head. "Okay. Why FWB instead of traditional relationships?"

"Oh. That's easy. I like sex, and I like calling my own shots."

He reattached the headliner. "Fair enough. Would you like to come over?"

A small smile played on her lips as she reached over and placed her hand on his knee, sliding it down his inner thigh.

Daniel startled for a second, then held her gaze with a light behind his eyes before returning his attention to the headliner and bracket.

"Everything's right where it needs to be. Looks like I'm on top of my game today."

Aubrey smiled and held out her hand, helping him out of the backseat.

Daniel pulled Aubrey close in his dark bedroom, breathing in the scent of her hair right under his nose. He didn't know he was going to see her today let alone invite her over. But her in her T-shirt, form fitting jeans and boots put him in the mood quickly.

He planted a kiss on top of her head. "You know, plenty of men are fine with you calling your own shots even in traditional relationships."

"Plenty of men meaning you?"

"Yes, I happen to be one of them. Let's not forget, my chick just left the nest a few months ago. I don't want to run anyone's life but my own."

She stirred in his arms and turned, giving him a lingering kiss. "Then FWB is perfect for you." Another kiss. "I better get going. This was a very nice evening."

He pulled on the lounge pants and T shirt from last night and slipped on tennis shoes to walk her to her car.

His warm apartment seemed cooler and emptier when he returned. The gentle touch of paws on his knee turned his attention downward. Okay, only just a little emptier.

He picked Briscoe up and cuddled him. "Well Big B. Maybe she's right."

Aubrey stood up to greet Andrew when he entered the Deer Valley Terminal. "I'm so glad you were able to come flying today. Payson is beautiful this time of year, and you're going to love breakfast at Crosswinds."

They headed for her plane tied down on the tarmac. 30 minutes later, they were seated near a window overlooking the transient parking and the runway. A Beech Baron and a Cessna 172 were tied down in the parking area along with Aubrey's plane. The Mogollon Rim in the distance had a dusting of snow at the top.

Andew looked up and around at the model airplanes hanging from the ceiling. "Wow, there must be over 50 planes."

"Something like that. They are all donated from people's collections. When they pass on, and the family doesn't know what to do with so many models, some are donated to airports and restaurants like this." She motioned around the room. "Same with the pictures on the walls."

Aubrey took a sip of her coffee. "I've made a new friend recently. I'm getting concerned that he may develop feelings for me. He's new to the state, so he doesn't know a lot of people. Hence, he doesn't have any FWBs except me."

Andrew nodded. "That is risky. You know, I may be able to help you out. The sister of a good friend recently approached me. She's quite attractive, but I turned her down because, duh, she's my friend's sister."

Aubrey laughed. "If they're both open to it, we could share their contact information."

Daniel parked his truck after a parts run when an Asian guy walked toward the main parking lot from the terminal. Was he the guy Aubrey was with several months ago? Back when he thought she was taken. Well, she was, but she wasn't.

Daniel turned back to his truck. There were plenty of Asian guys around Deer Valley. Most of them from AeroGuard, and they wore pilot's uniforms. This guy was in street clothes. Moments later, the man got into a compact Toyota and headed for the exit.

He jerked the box containing the parts out of the bed of his truck. Did they just have sex in her hangar, or was it only a flight? It was none of his business. Who did she like better? Maybe neither of them. Someone else might be her favorite. Hell, he didn't even know if this was the same guy. He could be some guy who had lunch at Barrio Brewing Company.

Daniel carried the box past Justine's planters bursting with pink and red on the Skyways front patio.

Maybe he needed an FWB besides Aubrey. That would be two women he knew slept with other men. Still, it might be the distraction he needed.

Daniel had just stepped out of the shower when his phone chimed a facetime call. It was probably Mac. He let the call go, and a few minutes later, he heard a text chime. He'd call her back when he was decent.

The text and missed facetime were from Kathleen, the gal Aubrey told him about. He agreed to her giving the woman his contact information. He put on one of his nicer T-shirts and sweats, then combed his still-wet hair.

When he returned the call, an attractive woman with long, light brown hair with blonde highlights answered. She didn't look anything like Aubrey. Good.

Aubrey pressed the return button in her lane at C2 Tactical, bringing her target back to her. The bullet holes, which started near the center, were going in an upward direction. She sighed and shook her head. *Glad to be alone in this part of the range.*

"It's your stance."

She startled for a second and turned from her counter. Engrossed in her shooting, she didn't realize that Sonja had switched places with the red bearded man as the Range Safety Officer.

"Sorry. I can see you're frustrated." Her dark eyes were soft and friendly.

Aubrey sighed. "Yes, Daniel keeps telling me to lean forward. I just keep forgetting."

"Like everything else, it takes time."

Aubrey taped up the bullet holes in her target, then reattached it to the cardboard.

"Hang on a second. I have an idea." She motioned for the read-bearded employee to come in. "Warren, switch out her current rental for a Sig Sauer Rose."

Aubrey put the firearm back in its case and handed it to Warren.

"It's designed for women. I think you'll like it."

The firearm with the rose-gold accents seemed to fit her hands better. She loaded the magazine, then took on a more forward center of gravity.

"That's perfect. Just like that," Sonja said.

Aubrey slowly emptied the magazine, focusing on stance and aim. Her stomach fluttered, and she giggled when she saw the new set of bullet holes in more of a center cluster.

"Big difference, huh?" The other woman beamed.

"Yeah. Thanks."

"Hey, speaking of Daniel, are you two a thing?"

Her heart quickened. Daniel comes here all the time and talks to her. Lying would do no good. Why should she lie anyway? It wasn't her style. Not only that, she was also trying to set him up with Kathleen. What would it matter if Sonja became another "friend"? After all, Aubrey didn't want Daniel developing feelings for her. But what if she became a girlfriend instead of an FWB? Kathleen wanted an FWB. What did Sonja want?

"I'm sorry. I'm prying." Sonja put up a hand.

"No, no. It's okay. We're friends. We've become good friends since he moved here."

"Okay. I was just curious. Keep after it on the shooting. You're doing great." She signaled for Warren to come in and they switched places.

Just curious? Right.

The day was perfect for the annual Walk for the Animals and Adopt-a-Thon at Margaret T. Hance Park. Downtown Phoenix was sunny and cool. Daniel had heard about the event and invited Aubrey to go with him. She said she was working that day. Rochelle readily accepted when he invited her.

After walking several laps around the sprawling green park, Daniel offered to treat Rochelle to lunch at one of the food vendors. When they found a bench in the sun, near the Circle of Flags, Rochelle went to buy two Ben and Jerry's Doggie Desserts from another vendor. The small dogs pounced on their canine ice creams.

"Rochelle, I've been doing a lot of thinking lately."

"About?"

"Relationships. I'm not ready for a commitment right now."

She smiled. "I can understand that. You're an empty nester. Albeit a young one. You're enjoying your freedom. My divorce just became final six months ago. I'm not ready to commit either."

"Someone recently introduced me to friends with benefits. What do you think of arrangements like that?"

Her eyes turned to granite. "Are you asking me to be in a relationship like that with you? If you are, that's a hard no."

"Oh shit. No, I didn't mean.... I meant I wanted your opinion on friends with benefits because I'm not sure if it's for me."

Her shoulders lowered, and her eyes softened. "Okay... Good. Look, I'll just lay it out for you. I always felt used by my ex in the bedroom. Then when I found out about his multiple affairs, I realized he used all of us."

"I'm sorry." He reached up to touch her shoulder, then dropped his hand onto his thigh.

"When I packed up Rufus and left, I decided I would never just be another man's fun."

He looked into her face and held her gaze. "I can understand that. You shouldn't compromise on what you want."

"I won't." She reached down to pick up the Doggie Dessert containers before looking into his eyes. "I can't tell you what to do, but I say don't allow yourself to be her fun. Require more."

Chapter Seventeen

Aubrey wheeled her grocery cart from Basha's to her car. Music and conversation emanated from The Burg Sports Grill at the east end of the parking lot. As usual, there were several motorcycles parked out front.

He phone chimed. "Hey, Justine. What's up?"

Her heart sped up. Justine was crying. "It's Ken Leftson. His plane had some kind of engine trouble. He went down in the trees just north of Prescott. He...he didn't survive."

Aubrey clutched the cart, feeling weakness come over her. "When?"

"Within the last few hours. Nate and I are closing down for the day to drive to Prescott with Ginny."

After ending the call, Aubrey took some deep, calming breaths while gazing at the cloudless sky toward Prescott.

Ken. One of Nate's best friends. He was on the Publications Committee of the Deer Valley Pilot's Association. He made the board meetings fun with his jokes and harmless pranks. The monthly newsletter had a certain flair with him in charge of it.

Tears stung her eyes. Not Ken.

The ER at Banner Desert Medical Center was busy on a Saturday afternoon. Busy enough to keep Aubrey from crying over Ken's untimely passing a few days ago. Now that she sat alone at one of the outdoor dining areas, a few tears trickled down her cheeks. Pilots died flying for three reasons: pilot error, flying in bad weather, or mechanical failure. The weather had been perfect, and Skyways kept Ken's Piper Apache in top shape, just like they did her Romeo. What the hell happened with that airplane?

Aubrey had just returned from lunch when she entered the curtained off room and saw the familiar face of one of her cousins along with a man she didn't recognize.

"Hey there, Blaine."

"Aubrey! Great to see you. Are you going to do my stitches?" He took off the flannel that had a tear down the right sleeve, leaving him in a black T-shirt.

"Yep."

"This is Manny, my supervisor."

After shaking hands with him, Aubrey turned back to Blaine. "Would you like a local anesthetic?"

"Please. This thing hurts like hell." He motioned to the long cut on his arm.

Aubrey glanced at the paperwork. The cut came from a mishap caring for a horse at his job on one of the local Mesa ranches.

She retrieved the correct syringe and injected the anesthetic in the seventeen-year-old's forearm just above the cut.

"We'll give that a few minutes to take effect. How is your senior year going?"

"It's great. Busy but great."

"And Aunt Ginger and Uncle Raymond?"

"Mom and Dad are good. They always mention that they miss you during the holidays, though."

"I miss them too. I definitely miss Aunt Ginger's dressing and sweet potatoes."

"Still awesome. Also, are you and Uncle Franklin still not speaking?"

"Still not."

Aubrey retrieved the equipment from the tray by the bedside and began the stitches.

"Okay. I just wondered because when we all got together for my dad's birthday a few months ago, Uncle Franklin seemed different."

"Really, like how?" She paused her stitching for a second, then quickly resumed.

"First, he asked how my job was going and said he was glad I enjoyed working with the horses. Usually, he just complains that I shouldn't be working with animals. Instead, I should be getting a jump start on college."

"Interesting."

"Yeah. Then later he complimented the meal rather than mentioning a place that could have catered the party."

"You love horses, and Aunt Ginger loves to cook." Aubrey finished stitching.

"Yeah. I could tell my father was this close to asking if he had gotten therapy." He held his thumb and index finger on his opposite hand a centimeter apart. "Of course, he knew better than to do that."

Aubrey laughed. "Yes, but if anyone could get away with it, it would be Uncle Raymond."

My dad in therapy? Aubrey shook her head.

The large but somber group exited the small, multi-purpose building at Christ's Church of the Valley where Ken and his family had been members. Daniel had seen Ken a few times and talked to him once. Mainly Daniel was there for Nate. Nate shut down Skyways for the afternoon so everyone could attend Ken's celebration of life. Apparently, Aubrey knew him pretty well since they were both active in the Deer Valley Pilot's Association. Daniel stood with her while she took a moment to tearfully offer her condolences to the fellow pilot's wife, Ginny, and their three grown children.

Everyone gathered on the large, sprawling green lawn surrounded by various tan, red, and stone buildings to await the fly-over which Nate and Justine would be a part of. Aubrey was not going from person to person or group to group like she usually did, even though many in attendance were airport regulars.

"Wanna go sit out for a bit? It'll take a while for the fly-over to get ready."

She only nodded and walked over to the stairs leading to the second floor of a tan building labeled Teen Center. He put an arm around her and just sat with her. He had learned from his daughter and previous relationships that sometimes a gal just needed him to be there.

She leaned against him. "I'm sorry."

He pulled her a little closer. "For what?"

"For lying to you."

"I'm not sure what you mean, but it's okay."

"You asked why I do FWB."

"Yeah."

"It's true I like to call my own shots. And I really do love sex. But the truth is, when you give your heart to a man, they don't handle it with care. They think it's theirs to do what they want with."

He pulled her close again and planted a kiss on top of her head. "You deserve someone who will treat your heart with the same respect and care you show others."

He could be hiding in plain sight.

Aubrey was drying her hair when she heard the Ring doorbell chime. She picked up her cell phone to access the camera. In seconds, she recognized the casual but expensively dressed man on her doorstep.

She let out her breath in an annoyed huff and hit the answer button. "Yes?"

"Aubrey, we really need to talk."

He hadn't tried to contact her since Nate talked with him at Skyways a little over a month ago. She took a few moments to think.

She looked at his image on camera. He had lost weight. Her conversations with Blaine and Daniel ran through her head.

She looked again at the image. He said nothing, but she could hear him let out his breath. His shoulders slumped. "I understand." He turned and headed down her front walk.

"Damn it!" She shook her head and threw on her robe, then jerked open her front door.

"Dad...wait."

He had just reached his SUV when he stopped and turned.

Aubrey studied her father in silence for a moment. His face was more lined than before. He clearly tried to dress down, but his collared pullover, slacks and jacket were not purchased at Target or Walmart. His eyes held the hope and caution of a man who knew he would probably be rejected.

"Come in. You're going to have to give me a minute to get dressed."

He squared his shoulders. "Thank you."

Once in her bedroom, she retrieved a pair of lavender joggers and matching jacket along with a pink t-shirt.

What the hell was she doing? Last time they talked was her eighteenth birthday. She was worried one of the neighbors would call the police because the yelling was so loud.

She put her still damp hair into a quick French braid and headed down the hall.

Her father stood up from the overstuffed chair when she entered the living room. "Aubrey, can I take you to lunch? Just lunch and talking. Then I'll leave you alone."

She glanced at her phone. "It's a little early, but we should leave right away to beat the after-church crowd. What did you have in mind?"

"You choose."

This caused a start to course through her, which she hoped did not show.

Daniel stepped out of the shower and ran a comb through his wet hair after toweling off. Kathleen had called yesterday morning offering to meet somewhere today. He had put her off long enough. It was time to meet if he was going to at all. Her job in real estate kept her sporadically busy seven days a week. He figured he'd better jump at the chance when she had a free Sunday afternoon. Today, he and Kathleen would enjoy the Martin Auto Museum, talk, and maybe take it further.

After pulling on jeans and a tan long-sleeved pullover, he turned to Briscoe, who was lounging among the pillows on the comforter.

"Well Big B, how do I look?"

The dog wagged his tail.

The wait at Barrio Queen at Desert Ridge Marketplace was relatively short as they arrived right before the restaurant opened for lunch. They were seated near the cabinet that displayed a variety of tequila bottles.

Once seated, Aubrey took a moment to peruse the menu before deciding on grilled fish tacos with ranch beans.

She had noticed that her father was thinner than she had seen him a few years ago at a family wedding. He now ordered a meatless chopped salad with oil and vinegar.

Can't eat like a king forever. Even if you think you are one.

Once the server left, he turned his attention completely on Aubrey, folding his hands and resting them on the table.

"I know you're wondering why I have been trying to contact you out of nowhere."

She nodded.

"First, you need to know that I am not terminally ill and there is nothing I want from you."

"That's a start."

"I'm selling my half of Cassen and Harper Enterprises."

"Oh? That's been your life since before I came along. Are you sure everything is alright?"

"Positive. I'm going to take some time off and figure out my next move. One night several months ago, I sat on my back patio drinking my usual rum and Coke, now Diet Coke, and I started thinking about how my life was supposed to be. The only sounds I heard were my own breathing and the nocturnal sounds of the insects and birds. That's when I realized how alone I really was and how much I tried to control everyone around me to avoid this moment. Other than my company, what do I have?"

"I don't know, Dad."

Their food arrived, and Aubrey picked up one of her tacos. Her father left his salad untouched while he continued.

"Listen, Aubrey, as I said, after today's lunch, I don't expect you to ever see or talk to me again if you don't want to. I'll stay out of your life. I just wanted to have the chance to tell you that I see my mistake in thinking you were here for me. You're not here to live the life I wanted for you; you are here to build your own life. I was supposed to support you in that endeavor, and I didn't. I've heard you are happy with your life, and that's enough for me."

Halfway through her tacos, Aubrey took a sip of her iced tea. Her father had never admitted a mistake. She took another sip without saying anything. He had started eating his salad without looking at her.

"I'll be right back. Really." She got up and walked past the fireplace adorned with a red painted skull toward the bathroom.

His whole demeanor had changed since she last saw him. This was either a very good manipulation or something really had clicked with him. The memory of Daniel and Mackenzie in the booth at Manuel's came back to her like it was yesterday. They had such ease and affection. Aubrey was amazed at their openness. Daniel was one reason she stopped her father from driving off this morning. Of course, her relationship with her father could never be what Daniel and Mackenzie had, but could they have something?

She finished washing her hands and returned to their table where her dad was asking the server for a box. He looked the server in the face and nodded and smiled at something she said. Servers in restaurants were like everyone else in his life: they were there to serve him. Aubrey was often embarrassed when she would go out with him during her teen years. He tipped well, but they deserved it after dealing with him.

Aubrey smiled at the server as she walked past her.

"How were your tacos?" he asked when she sat down.

"Good." She took another long sip of her tea.

She looked her father square in the eye. "Lunch once a month. I'm willing to start with that and see what happens. No promises."

His eyes widened for a second, and he took a moment to swallow. "No promises expected."

He paid the check, leaving a good tip.

When Daniel parked his truck, Kathleen was already waiting for him at the front entrance between pillars. One pillar held the American flag and the other the Arizona flag. Their Facetime conversations over the last few weeks had been light and fun. She was beautiful too. When she suggested meeting at the auto museum, he knew he had won the trifecta.

"Hey. Nice to finally meet in person." She enveloped him in a friendly hug. "You're going to love this place. You can sit in most of the cars."

Her jeans and sky blue button down emphasized her figure without being too obvious. Sky blue. Aubrey's favorite color.

They entered the expansive showroom surrounded by auto related neon signs high up on the walls.

"So, did you grow up here?"

"No, I'm an Airforce brat. I lived on Luke Airforce Base during my late elementary years. After high school, I decided I wanted to go to college out here. Been here ever since."

They walked down a line of Cadillacs representing various years, colors, and body styles.

"What's your story? I know you moved here recently from Montana. Did you live there your whole life?"

"Yep. Born and raised. It was a great place to grow up, and a great place to raise my daughter."

"And you were a state trooper."

"Yes. For the most part, I loved it. I guess I'll start at the beginning. I grew up in Great Falls. Played baseball and wrote for the school newspaper in high school. Jen, my ex-wife, was an editor for the paper. In fact, our first conversation was an argument about an article I wrote."

Kathleen laughed. They entered a room set aside for Corvettes.

"I asked her out a few days later. I chose to become a state trooper since I really didn't want to work in the city. I also knew it would be somewhat safer since I had Mackenzie to think about. Once Jen got her two-year degree and found a job, I went to the Montana Law Enforcement Academy. I stayed at Jens' uncle's place in Helena during the week and went home on weekends. By the time Mackenzie was three, we both knew the marriage was over. We still had our daughter to raise so we worked out a not perfect but very good co-parenting arrangement."

"Great Falls. I lived at Malmstrom Air Base for a while. I was pretty young. Don't remember much about it." Kathleen stopped at a T-38 Mini Jet in the middle of the Corvette room and bent down to look at the gauges.

His groin tightened while his eyes followed the curve of her buttocks. He looked away right as she straightened. A slight grin curved her lips.

After the Corvette room, they walked around a circular section of high-speed vehicles including a black Dodge Challenger next to a shiny blue Charger. He stopped and looked them over. *Aubrey.*

"You really like those cars, don't you? Come over here, I'll show you one of my favorites."

She led him past a miniature carousel to a bright yellow 1955 Studebaker. "This was the first year an eight cylinder engine was an option."

She slid into the back seat and motioned to Daniel to do the same. When he joined her in the spacious back seat, she leaned against him.

"I've always wondered what it would be like to do it in the back of a vintage car."

He pulled her a little closer. "Maybe you'll get your chance one day."

By the time they finished walking the rows of mostly American makes and models, it was early evening. They decided to grab a quick, light dinner nearby. The server brought the check to Daniel's side of the table, but Kathleen insisted they split the bill. When the server left with the check and credit cards, Kathleen's smile took on a serious look.

"Daniel, would you like to come over to my place?"

After lunch, Aubrey took her jeep to her favorite mesa. A little four-wheeling and solitude looking out over the city would calm her churned up emotions. She was glad she accepted her father's lunch invitation. But did she want to be glad? Everything about her was all about him. Now, after thirty years he realized his mistake.

Her phone rang. *Carmella.*

The moment Aubrey answered, her friend's voice gushed through the phone. "I'm engaged! Brock proposed last night. We drove up to South Mountain after dinner at the Biltmore. He got down on one knee while we overlooked the city lights below."

"Carmella, that's wonderful! You've been waiting a little while for this."

"I have. You know I said yes immediately. Of course, I want you to be my maid of honor. It's going to be a traditional Mexican wedding. Wear your dancing shoes and don't plan on going to bed that night...Aubrey?"

"I'm so happy for you." She blinked back tears.

"I know you are, but you don't sound like I imagined you would. What's going on?"

Aubrey gazed at the Phoenix skyline off in the distance. "I had lunch with my father a few hours ago."

"Whoa! Tell me everything."

No? ... No? Daniel parked his truck in its parking space.

He and Kathleen had had a wonderful afternoon together ending with dinner and a guaranteed invitation for sex. No? ... When the rubber met the road, he couldn't go through with it.

He knew she was disappointed but accepted his answer gracefully.

<h1 style="text-align:center;">Chapter Eighteen</h1>

Daniel and Aubrey entered The Buckeye Air Fair, an event that drew in many pilots and their families every year. Aubrey stopped often at the booths and chatted up the airshow pilots, YouTube stars, and people who sold aviation related gadgets and products. She made a point to introduce him to everyone she knew.

Briscoe happily sniffed the weeds and rocks on the flat dirt and asphalt but remained cautious when people approached.

As they canvassed Buckeye Airport, she turned to him. "I had lunch with my father a week ago."

"Really!? How was it?"

"Surprisingly nice. We're planning another lunch sometime this month. I'm still on my guard. I don't know if anything has actually changed or if this is a guise. If it's a guise, he can't keep it up month after month. Can it really be that he realized his mistake?"

"Well. A few years after our divorce, Jen got remarried to a mutual friend. Mac was five at the time. Wyatt has always been great with kids, so I knew he would be good to her. What I didn't count on was how I would feel when Mackenzie started gushing about him and I started seeing them interact. My attitude changed. I became competitive with Wyatt. Who was going to be the better dad? The problem was, my time with my daughter became more about one-upping him rather than being a good father. One Saturday, we spent an entire day together trying to make her love the activities and meals I had planned. Some she was okay with. Others she hated, which pissed me off. That night about an hour after I had put her to bed, I walked by her room and heard her crying. I felt this big."

Daniel held his thumb and index finger a centimeter apart.

"When I went in to talk to her, she poured out everything she had been feeling for over a year. She talked about how she loved me, but she also loved Wyatt, but she felt like I didn't want her to love him, and she couldn't choose. Of course, I'm paraphrasing. She was explaining all of this in seven-year-old terms."

Aubrey nodded.

"My point is, I realized what an asshole I had been and how my male pride was hurting my daughter. I'm not telling you what to do concerning your father. I learned my lesson about that."

Aubrey laughed.

"I am saying it's possible that it's just what he said. He realized his mistake and now a relationship with you is what's important, not his image." Daniel zipped his hoodie. "But, yes, take it slowly, like you said."

After a quick barbecue dinner on a cooling patio, Daniel parked in front of Aubrey's house. His eyes traced the contour of her profile as she reached for her purse on the floorboards. There was that familiar stirring in his groin.

Aubrey glanced at the dashboard. "Forty degrees. The weatherman wasn't kidding about the cold front moving in this evening."

Daniel shrugged. "This isn't bad compared to what I'm used to this time of year."

She looked into his face and seemed to read his thoughts. She then gave him a 'come hither' look. "Either way, can I interest you in a hot shower?" She held out her hand.

He smiled, exiting his truck and taking the hand she offered. Once inside, Briscoe now accustomed to Aubrey's house, jumped onto her couch and curled up among the pillows.

Aubrey shed her fleece, top, and bra, carrying them down the short hall to the hamper. Daniel waited until he reached her bedroom to yank off his sweatshirt and the T-shirt underneath. Her eyes sparkled as she stood topless scanning his shirtless form. His pants were now way too restrictive. He quickly unfastened them. By the time he was fully undressed, Aubrey was only in tan satin panties.

She turned the water on, then turned sideways to him, gave him a smile, slid the panties down her legs and stepped out of them.

Daniel crossed into the bathroom and closed the door.

She adjusted the hot and cold water. "This is a perfect temperature for me. Let me know if it's too much one way or the other."

He stuck his foot out into the cascading water, then stepped fully in. "Perfect for me too," he said before putting his face and head under the shower stream.

Aubrey took her turn wetting her hair and body. Daniel began rubbing her lemongrass shampoo between his palms.

He gave her a wry smile. "Turn around."

The shower stream ran down the front of her as Daniel massaged her scalp, then worked the shampoo down to the ends of her hair. He reached around, tipping up her chin before detaching the showerhead. The warmth of her wet hair trailed down his chest. After replacing the showerhead, he pulled her to him, taking in the feel of her back and buttocks against his chest and groin.

Aubrey stepped away, grabbing her bottle of citrus and spice body wash, then retrieved a shower chair from outside the plexiglass enclosure. "Have a seat."

In seconds, he was seated and taking in the creamy lather across his chest and down his arms. He closed his eyes and tipped his head back as she worked her way to his thighs and down to his feet. The pressure in his groin was nearly painful, but he didn't want to rush.

The sound of a wrapper tearing brought another surge. *It wouldn't be long now.* After quickly sheathing him, she settled herself onto him, first remaining still, clenching and releasing him. Holding back was getting more and more difficult by the second. When she started slowly moving, he squeezed some body wash onto his hands and began slowly massaging the liquid onto her belly and breasts. Her quick breaths became cries as his hands repeatedly caressed her tight nipples. He couldn't hold back any longer. Her impassioned gaze held his as he bucked and exploded inside her. He pulled her to him, not sure he had the strength to move.

He didn't know how long they stayed like that, but her nipples against his chest and the rate of her breathing said she hadn't come yet. He stirred beneath her, and she climbed off. He again detached the shower head and rinsed her. Readjusting the stream, he pulled her back to his chest and guided the stream to where her legs joined.

"Pressure okay?"

"Perfect."

That seemed to be all she could say until her body against him tensed and she loudly cried out.

The next hour or so, they cuddled under Aubrey's flower-sprayed comforter talking until sleepiness seemed to overcome her. Everything in him wanted to stay under the comforter and just hold her. She likely wouldn't appreciate waking up with him still there. He slipped out of bed and redressed. She stirred sightly and gave a quiet acknowledgement when he kissed the top of her head before he headed down the hallway.

Chapter Nineteen

Daniel set out the napkins, paper plates, and plasticware on the kitchen table. The beers, sodas, and bottled water were in the cooler. Everything was ready for his first Super Bowl party in Arizona. Ricardo and Gabrielle were bringing tortilla chips and dip made from chorizo. Ray and Vanessa were bringing wings that were a specialty of Ray's. Aubrey was bringing chili. Daniel had recently met another single guy in his complex who had moved to Phoenix from Atlanta for work. Steve said he would bring a variety of chips and dips.

Nate and Justine had other plans, and Sasha and her new boyfriend didn't watch any sports.

Daniel secured Briscoe in his bedroom knowing the pup would be more comfortable. Nowadays, he left the crate open at all times, allowing Briscoe to use it as den when he wanted or needed to. Later, he would open the bedroom door and give him the choice of where he wanted to be.

The doorbell started ringing. Steve arrived first, and as the others trickled in, Daniel introduced him.

Aubrey was the last to arrive with a crockpot full of the same chili she brought to the Christmas potluck. The aroma sent a surge through him as images of Aubrey in her hangar that night came vividly back.

Daniel shook away the memory and made sure his guests had what they needed. By the start of the game, everyone had filled their plates and found a spot in front of the large screen television.

When the game ended, most of the food had been eaten. Two full trash bags sat on the kitchen floor. Slowly, the guests left. Daniel fed Briscoe while Aubrey washed her crockpot.

When Daniel returned from his second trip to the dumpster, he grabbed Briscoe's leash.

"Thank you for your help cleaning up. Just lock the door manually when you leave, I can unlock it with the app."

"Okay," she called over her shoulder.

When he returned, Aubrey was sitting on the couch looking a little green. "Hey. You okay?"

"I think I misjudged how much I ate and drank. It just kind of hit me while I was doing dishes."

"What do you need?"

She placed her hand on her abdomen. "Just a ride home."

With the window of her challenger down, Aubrey took some deep breaths, helping clear her head and settle the nausea. "So, did Mackenzie ever come home drunk?"

"Yep. She was fifteen and staying the night at a friend's house. Her friend's mom went out for a few hours, and they decided to sample the liquor cabinet."

"Oh no."

"The mom called me right away when she came home."

"How much trouble was she in?"

"Plenty. Once she slept it off and I helped her manage her hangover, she got a big lecture about the risks of being young, female, and drunk. Granted, she did her experiment in the safety of her friend's house, but I didn't want it to become a habit."

"Sounds like you handled it better than my father did. He blew his stack about how people were going to talk after seeing me drunk at a big high school party."

"He probably worried about the danger you were in, just wasn't in touch with it."

"Maybe. My friend Carmela's older brother got me home safely." A giant wave of nausea came over her. "Pull over!"

Daniel jerked the car to the side of the road.

Once at her house, Daniel helped her in and to bed.

"I'll pay for your Uber home."

"Don't worry about that right now."

The last thing she felt was a kiss on her forehead.

She woke the next morning with a headache and a very dry mouth. *Hydrate. You'll feel better.*

She stumbled down the hall past pictures of family and friends to find Daniel at her kitchen table scrolling on his phone. Her heart melted.

He stood up. "What can I get you?"

"All I want right now is green tea and dry toast."

"Sit down. I'll get it for you." He handed her a bottle of water from the fridge.

She gingerly sipped the water while instructing Daniel on where to find the tea and bread. "I thought you took an Uber home."

He yawned. "Couldn't. I was worried about you, so I slept on your couch checking on you every few hours. That's not breaking any rules, is it?" His mouth turned up in a slight smirk.

She smiled up at him when he handed her the mug of tea and set down the plate of toast. "No. It's fine. Thank you."

When Daniel left to attend to Briscoe and get ready for work, Aubrey basked in the fleeting warmth of Daniel's presence in her house. She wasn't hung over often, but when she was, she was always on her own. She sipped her tea focusing on the door Daniel just exited. Her eyes then found the snow-themed throw blanket on her couch. Daniel had folded it differently than she did. Aubrey took a small bite of her toast. *This was wonderful, but don't get too used to it.*

The sun was just setting on a Tuesday evening when Aubrey finished washing and waxing her plane in the north hangars' wash rack. Her phone chimed indicating a facetime call. Her father.

She hit the accept button. "Hi."

"Hi. I hope I'm not disturbing you, but I wanted to find out when you wanted to have lunch this month. If you still want to."

"Yes, I still do. I will work a day shift tomorrow but a night shift on Thursday so I can be available for lunch. Does Thursday work for you, or do you need more notice?"

Aubrey turned toward the rows of planes tied down in transient parking in front of the large hangars. A coyote trotted between transient parking and the taxiway, quickly heading to the desert east of the hangars.

"I'll make sure I'm free.... I see you're at the airport. I've seen a couple of pictures of your plane from when you took Aunt Ginger flying."

"Oh, I'll give you the tour." She switched to her back camera on her phone.

Starting at the tip of the right wing, she slowly walked around the plane. She then ascended the wing and showed him the interior and avionics, explaining the gauges and how she used each GPS.

"Your flying lessons always made you so happy. You seemed to glow after every flight."

"It's my first love."

"Well, I'm grateful Nate used his connections to help you get your plane."

An awkward silence followed. After Aubrey chose a place for them to meet, she taxied the plane to her hangar.

Her father's comment about her flying lessons rang in her head. Even in the worst of their arguments, he never threatened to cancel any of her flying lessons.

Aubrey had just stepped out of a child's room on the OR recovery floor when she saw Chad come out of a closet at the end of one hallway. She slipped into another child's room, so he walked right by her. By the time she finished taking vitals and came out of the room, a dark-haired nurse exited the same closet looking right then left. Aubrey walked by her, glanced at her nametag, and gave her a knowing look. The woman met Aubrey's gaze, also glancing at Aubrey's nametag. She was not as young as she looked from a distance.

Eight years ago, she had been that nurse. They never had sex in those closets, but there were plenty of hot make-out sessions. Anger rose from her chest. Bile burned her throat. Chad was divorced now, and his new flame was making her own choices. This was none of her business.

Aubrey went about her duties which included seeing one of Chad's latest patients. The child was healing up nicely. From what Aubrey had heard, Chad was one of the best orthopedic surgeons in the region. Mid shift, Aubrey stopped at her borrowed locker. Chad's closet nurse walked into the break room. *None of your business.* Aubrey quickly scanned the room. *None of your business.* They were alone. *Damn it! Here goes.*

"Hi. Katie, right?"

The other woman turned; recognition washed over her face. Her eyes hardened.

"Yes, and you're Aubrey. I mentioned our little exchange in the hallway to Dr. Hartshorn. He said you two have a past and that you might talk shit about him."

Aubrey's heart sped up a little. "Well, he doesn't know me as well as he thinks he does. Sorry to bother you."

Her look softened. "I appreciate your concern. Really. But I can take care of myself."

Aubrey made a quick exit without being too obvious. Judging by her patients, Katie wasn't a pediatric nurse, so they could probably avoid each other.

When Aubrey got to her car that evening, she texted Carmella. Her friend had a late meeting and wasn't available. Justine wouldn't be available either as she and Nate went country dancing on Wednesday nights. She called Daniel, then drove directly to his apartment.

Daniel opened his front door before she reached it. "Hey, on the phone you sounded like you were ready to demolish a brick wall. What's going on?"

She sat on his couch and picked up Briscoe and just held him for a moment. Did she really want to tell Daniel this?

"Well, I guess it's time for the whole humiliating story."

Daniel brought her a box of tissues.

Her shining eyes met his. His eyes only held concern. "I was twenty-two and had only been a nurse for a few years. I had just gotten a job in the ER at Arizona General Hospital. A surgical resident ten years my senior started paying a lot of attention to me. Of course, we kept everything below the radar. He promised me a great life with him once he finished his residency. I was all ready to move to wherever he got hired. One day, a pregnant woman brought in her preschooler who was running a fever. When I went to triage the kid, I saw the last name on the chart. It was same uncommon last name as Chad's, my knight in shining armor. Then I looked at the father's name on the chart. Bingo! Shortly after that, he finished his residency and took his happy family to Houston."

Fresh tears coursed down her cheeks. Daniel handed her a tissue but wiped her tears with another. He then gently pulled her close and just held her.

"They're divorced now. Chad moved back here, and now he found a new nurse to exploit. He's probably going to do her like he did me, then move on to the next one."

"Okay. I understand you don't want what happened to you to happen to anyone else. Unfortunately, you don't have any control over that."

"So, my stupid decision is just my stupid decision."

"In a word, yes, but I'm not sure you did what you did out of stupidity. Look Aubrey, you're not the first idealistic young woman to fall in love with the wrong guy. You won't be the last no matter what you do."

She shook her head. "So, the best I can do is make sure it doesn't happen to me again? Mission accomplished."

"Yes, mission accomplished. Not because of your FWB lifestyle, but because of your judge of character. I've seen the way you interact with different people on and off the airport. You read people and respond to them accordingly. If you ever do choose one man, he's going to be someone worth it."

Someone worth it. She leaned against his chest.

Aubrey arrived a little out of breath at Hillstone Restaurant, near her father's office. He had always worked in the business and culinary district known as the Camelback Corridor. Franklin was already seated near one of the large windows looking out onto a shaded courtyard.

"Sorry I'm late. Accident on the 51." She picked up her menu and began perusing it.

"You seem in a hurry. Do you have somewhere to be?"

"No, but I figured you probably have meetings today, and I'm already fifteen minutes late."

"I rescheduled any meetings I had for today, so take your time ordering." Her shoulders relaxed, and she leaned against the booth.

This will take some getting used to

Once the server took their order, Franklin turned to Aubrey. "So, what all is happening in your life?"

"Well, I'm sure you heard that I do fill-in nursing. Pediatrics. I love it. I use my plane to move animals to and from shelters and rescues. You remember my friend Carmela?"

He nodded.

"She's engaged. She's a corporate controller and he's a CFO. Actually, they both work here in the Corridor like you do. I'm going to be maid of honor at the wedding."

"That's wonderful. I always knew Carmella was going places."

Aubrey's stiffened, and her stomach clenched.

His direct gaze met hers. "What I mean is she accomplished the goals she had for herself. Just like you did."

"You should know that I've decided not to get married or have kids."

The memory of Daniel holding her on his couch the previous night caused a dull ache in her chest.

Her father looked down and adjusted the napkin on his lap when their food arrived. "I don't blame you. You didn't exactly have the best example."

They picked at their meals in silence for a few moments. Then Franklin looked up and smiled.

"It was great seeing your plane the other night. I'd love to hear more about your flying."

Aubrey laughed. "Well, in that case, it's a good thing you don't have any meetings today."

Chapter Twenty

Aubrey pulled the throttle back on the Bonanza's engine. The alternating green and white beacon of Deer Valley Airport was in sight, glowing against the early dusk. She punched in the numbers 126.5 for the ADIS frequency, hit the toggle switch, then listened to the current recorded message, information Tango.

Next, she punched in the frequency for the control tower. "Deer Valley Tower Bonanza 6282 Romeo coming in from the north with Tango for a full stop."

"82 Romeo, report when you are at the canal and freeway."

"Report canal and freeway, 82 Romeo."

The intersecting snakes of the I-17 freeway and Salt River Project's Grand Canal came into view. "Deer Valley Tower November 6282 Romeo at canal and freeway."

"82 Romeo, make right traffic for runway 25 Right. You are second behind a Sirus cleared to land."

She looked out her window in the direction her traffic GPS indicated. "Traffic in sight. Cleared to land 25 Right, 82 Romeo."

Aubrey looked down at her gauges and repeated her mental checklist.

Gas, undercarriage, mixture, prop, gear is down.

Once she landed and pushed her plane back in the hangar, she jumped into her Challenger with a plan to head home and heat up a can of beef stew. On the way to the exit gate, she caught sight of Marlon's hanger down row 42. It was open and lit. As he noticed her and waved, his white hair seemed to glow in the setting sun.

She pulled up and rolled down her window as he approached. "Packing it in for today?"

"Yeah, just went to Gila Bend for some cheap fuel. You?"

"Just got back from Knab, Utah. I took three pit bull mixes to an animal sanctuary out there."

"Best Friends?"

"That's the one."

"Very nice. Hey, would you like to come to my place for some sandwiches?"

An evening with Marlon seemed just the thing for tonight.

Aubrey sat down at the small table in the breakfast nook of Marlon's home north of the airport. She watched him through the archway leading into his kitchen. Marlon was from Chicago and made a healthy, home-made version of Italian beef sandwiches. No one who tried them missed the fat and salt. They were often his contribution to the airport's potluck lunches. She took a moment to savor her first bite.

"Good?"

"Always. How are you doing? And I mean really."

"I'm good, Aubrey, really. I find things to do and stay active every day. I've adjusted to living alone. Thanks to you and the others, I'm in better shape than I've ever been."

Aubrey and Marlon had been platonic friends at the airport for years. When his wife died of an unexpected heart attack, many at the airport rallied around him. Being a widower overnight jolted him into making some lifestyle changes. Aubrey and other current and retired medical professionals came alongside him and helped him build a healthier lifestyle. He lost weight, and his aging skin took on a healthy glow.

Aubrey ran into him about a year ago on the way out of Abrazo Health, Scottsdale, where he had just finished a cooking class. He said he had made a great meal that evening and really didn't want to eat it alone. That meal led to their first time having sex.

"That said, I'm glad you came over tonight. I was really feeling the loneliness right about the time you showed up."

"It's only been two, two and half years, and you had no time to prepare."

"Yes, two years, four months and six days." He looked down at his empty plate.

Aubrey's heart melted.

"They say to wait two years before making any big decisions regarding property or relationships, but I don't feel ready yet."

"If you're not ready, then you're not ready. Nothing wrong with that."

His eyes took on a faraway look. "What we had was so special. We told each other everything. We traveled the country so many times. Even went to Mexico and Canada a few times. I miss the inside jokes and special memories. The things that were uniquely us."

Aubrey took his hand when his eyes teared up.

"I just don't know if I can fall in love again after what we had, but I miss the companionship. My house is just so quiet sometimes."

Marlon headed down the hall toward his room. Aubrey picked up the condiments from the table and packed up the leftovers. She then took the dishes from the table and put them in the sink. Marlon's arms encircled her waist. She took in the spice of his Gravite cologne.

"I'll get the dishes in the morning, Aubrey." She relaxed against him as his hands moved up her abdomen, pulling her to him.

Daniel straddled his bike and started the engine. He had called Aubrey earlier that evening to see about dinner and some time in his bedroom. She didn't answer her phone. She was probably working or flying. Or with another friend. He shook his head before putting on his helmet.

A ride was just what he needed tonight. He guided his bike slowly through the curved parking lot to the exit gate. Tonight, he would head north to what Ray and other riders called the Sonora Desert Drive loop. He had taken it during the day a few times but wondered what it would be like at night. The wind pushed his coat against his arms and chest as the road gently meandered right and left past housing developments and high-end apartment complexes.

The last couple of weeks with Aubrey made his head spin. Aubrey, so beautiful, strong and capable. She would make any man a true partner in life. Any man? Him. She would make him a true partner.

After crossing the bridge over the canal, Daniel merged east onto Sonora Desert Drive. Housing developments adorned the desert to the south while an expanse of empty land spread out to the north. When the road narrowed from four lanes to two, the streetlights and housing developments disappeared. With his left hand, Daniel clicked on his high beams while watching for any wildlife that may dart out in front of him.

Aubrey's domineering father and a cheating lover caused her to use that strength as a shell to hide her vulnerability. Every protective cell in his body hummed when he held Aubrey as she cried on his shoulder, and when he put her to bed after the Superbowl. She was clearly surprised to see him still there the next morning.

The beautiful dark road continued to meander past benched overlooks for the hiking and mountain bike trails. The dark shapes of hills, saguaros, and various trees and bushes stood out against the night sky backlit by the lights of Phoenix.

Why couldn't Aubrey see that he would do right by her? Why did she need the others?

Off in the distance, the Kool radio antennas towered above the desert lights blinking red. Daniel clicked off his high beams when he approached Cave Creek Road. The light ahead was green. A thrill shot through him as he twisted the throttle, watching the tachometer jerk up. The bike gripped the road as he turned to the south, letting out a whoop. *Back to civilization.* He eased the throttle to a more reasonable speed.

After passing two cemeteries, Daniel merged right into the familiar industrial area east of the airport. When he stopped at the light across from the FBI building, Aubrey's Challenger passed in front of him heading toward her place. She didn't look in his direction, but he caught a quick glimpse of her. The heat of desire blended with a twinge of heartache.

Aubrey drove home replaying the evening's events. The full moon was high in the dark sky. Marlon was an excellent lover, and tonight was no exception. When he brought her to the peak of desire, it brought credence to the fact that the French word for orgasm translated to "the little death." So, what was the deal tonight? She had had a wonderful time and both she and Marlon were satisfied, yet something felt off.

Her last encounter with Daniel came to mind. The last time they were together it had been incredible. She hadn't wanted him to leave, but asking him to stay would have broken a hard and fast rule. What about the night he did stay? Not for sex, but out of concern for her. When she stumbled down her hallway, she found all the shades drawn, letting in muted light. He also kept his voice low. She wanted him to stay then too, but he was already going to be late to work that morning.

Tonight, she wanted to leave soon after she climbed off of Marlon and lay next to him in his candle lit bedroom. Basking in that warmth wasn't the same.

Aubrey helped set Daniel up with Kathleen. Maybe they had gotten together. They should have if it was going to work between them. Once Daniel got a couple of FWBs, he would be less available. She could enjoy him while getting back to the life she had before he disrupted it.

Chapter Twenty-One

The morning dawned cool and sunny. Daniel drove the fuel truck to the north hangars. He chose a route that took him past Aubrey's row of hangars. With her flexible schedule and unpredictable hours, she was as likely to be there as not.

This morning, he found her hangar door open and drove down the even side of Row 45. Aubrey was going through a preflight around the outside of her plane. He stopped and rolled down his window.

"Where are you headed this morning?" he asked.

"Going to Albuquerque to pick up a cargo of dogs from the Humane Society of the United States. They are destined for euthanasia, but Friends for Life has room for them, so I'm bringing them to Phoenix."

Daniel took in the sense of purpose on her face. "Are you free tomorrow night, or do you already have Valentine's Day plans?"

"I'm free."

"Great because I had some fish flown in from Montana. Dinner at my place at around 6:30?"

"You have fish flown in? The stores here sell fish, you know?"

Daniel shook his head. "Not the same and definitely not as good. Not as far as freshwater fish is concerned, anyway."

"In that case, I'll be there tomorrow at 6:30 sharp." She gave him a quick peck on the cheek and headed back to her plane.

After taking a moment to admire her from behind, he turned the truck around.

Aubrey entered Daniel's apartment to the smell of fish baking in the oven and potatoes frying on the stove.

"I think I'm going to like this."

"I hope so. I'm cooking the fish the same way several generations in my family have," Daniel said, stirring the potatoes, then taking them off the burner.

After greeting Briscoe and cuddling him for a moment, she turned to Daniel. "I need to let you know right away that I accepted a job at Phoenix Children's Hospital on the way here. I have to be there at 7:00 tomorrow morning so tonight needs to be just dinner."

He shrugged. "Okay."

When he finished dividing up the fried potatoes and steamed asparagus between the two plates, he took the trout out of the oven and placed one filet on each plate.

Aubrey savored two bites of the flaky fish baked in lemon, garlic, and olive oil. "You're right, this is better than any lake fish I've had here.

Daniel smiled. "Good. You should fly into Montana like you talk about sometimes."

"I will. But right now, I'm saving up time and money to go to Wisconsin for the EAA Airventure this summer. I haven't been in a few years, and I really miss it."

"I hear a lot of pilots talk about Oshkosh."

"Well, it's the aviation family reunion of the year. A pilot's dream world. They even have a little white chapel on the field where the stained glass is pictures of planes along with religious symbols."

"Are you planning to fly there?"

"No. Way too nerve-wracking. They have the best air traffic controllers in the nation in the tower that week, but still...."

Daniel took their plates to the kitchen sink and took a cherry cheesecake out of the refrigerator.

"Just curious. Have you talked to Kathleen?"

"Yeah. We had a nice afternoon together a while back, but when she invited me over.... It just didn't feel right."

"Sometimes it doesn't. It takes trial and error, especially at the beginning. After a time, you get a sense of who may or may not be a good FWB partner."

After helping Daniel with cleaning up, Aubrey glanced at the clock. She turned toward him, taking in his rugged features once again.

"Well, I hate to eat and run, but as I said, I really do have to go."

"I don't want to keep you too late." He pulled her to him, and his lips found hers.

A surge went through her as she pressed her body to his. "We keep that up, and I'll change my mind about it being too late."

"You need your rest." He leaned in for one more kiss. "Come on. I'll walk you to your car."

Daniel leashed Briscoe to take him on his walk. The evening had been perfect. Good food and wonderful company.

He zipped his hoodie against the cold night air and started walking down his usual path lit by solar-powered lights.

When she arrived, Aubrey seemed concerned about the fact that they weren't going to have sex tonight. Maybe because it was Valentine's Day. The thought had certainly crossed his mind. Sex between them was incredible, but he loved the time he spent with her no matter what they did. Then he cringed. She said trial and error was involved in FWB. How much trial and error had she done, anyway?

He sighed. This wasn't going to work if he couldn't handle her having other partners.

Aubrey made her rounds on a relatively quiet day at the pediatric ER triaging patients, starting IVs, and administering medication along with reassuring worried parents.

Break time. It was one of those February days that made everyone want to be in Arizona all winter. Lunch outside was definitely in order. Her conversation with Daniel a few nights ago came to mind. This summer, she would make it to Oshkosh. She needed to book an Air BnB and rental car soon. Visions of Wisconsin's beautiful green fields and meadows played through her memory. Daniel would probably love Oshkosh, or more likely, she would love to have him there with her. Out of town trips were the exception to her 'no overnights' rule. Problem was, Daniel wasn't taking to FWB very well. Feelings for her were not far behind. Spending a week in the same bed every night would only cement those feelings.

She exited the elevator and turned the corner when she froze in her steps. Chad and Katie sat eating at one of the courtyard tables, their heads drawn in close. Katie waved her left hand as she talked when the sun glinted off of something. A diamond or series of diamonds or both.

She turned quickly before they saw her and stormed down the hallway toward the cafeteria. Obviously, Chad wasted no time moving on with life. *One family crashes and burns, let's build another one right away.* He was her last exclusive relationship. She had moved on and rebuilt, just not in the traditional sense. Tears stung behind her eyelids. What would her life have been like had she not gotten involved with him?

Daniel was on top of his game at C2 on a Thursday evening after work. The target he bought had a nice cluster in the center. Now however, his range time was up, and the place was about to close.

Sonja looked to be starting her closing paperwork when Daniel collected his driver's license from the young blonde woman manning the counter. The blonde left to join fellow employees in straightening displays and end of evening cleaning. A small group of grizzled Vietnam Vets headed for the exit.

"You guys have a good night," she called out to them.

One touched the brim of his ball cap and nodded to her.

She smiled up at Daniel, seeming a little surprised he was still there. "How'd you do?"

"Great." He showed her the target, then lowered his voice. "About how long will it take you to finish up here?"

She gave him full eye contact. "Around twenty minutes. Why?"

"Frozen custard at Freddy's?"

Her eyes twinkled. "See you there."

After ordering a chocolate sundae and strawberry shake, they took a booth at the back of the red and white dining area. Daniel scanned the room and looked out the large windows before taking a sip of his shake. He should have ordered an ice water to go with it. The shake was doing little to ease his dry mouth.

"Your friend, the blonde gal, is making a lot of progress. She seems determined to learn to shoot well."

He had spent the evening getting Aubrey out of his head. Now Sonja brought her into the conversation. He pushed away the image of Aubrey and focused on Sonja's warm brown eyes and coal black hair held back by a pink clip.

"Yeah. She's determined alright. But if you don't mind, I'm not here to talk about her."

"Oh?" Sonja raised an eyebrow and leaned closer to him across the table. A small line of cleavage became visible at the top of her collared pullover.

Here goes.

"Well, since we met. I've noticed you've been sending signals."

"You're not wrong."

"I haven't responded since I don't think I'm ready for a relationship yet."

"Fair enough."

Daniel's heart quickened.

"I've been introduced to friends-with-benefits. I definitely find you attractive, and if you're open to it, I'd like to explore that type of relationship with you."

Her eyes went to the ceiling, and she tilted her head back and forth slightly. Daniel let out his breath after realizing he was holding it.

Sonja leaned in even closer. "My place isn't far from here, and my kids are with their father tonight."

Aubrey's cell phone rang as she was finishing her makeup. Daniel's voice on the other end made her smile.

"Are you working today?"

"No, I'm flying to Blythe, California to pick up some of their overflow and take them to County."

"I'm off today. Mind if I tag along?"

After a smooth flight, Aubrey and Daniel landed at Blythe Airport just west of the Arizona border. A representative from Riverside County Animal Control was there to meet them and took them to the organization's main campus.

When Aubrey handed Cindy the list of animals she was picking up, the director appeared flustered.

"Um...I'm sorry. There's been a mistake. I need to make a few phone calls." She shook her head.

"No problem. Can we take the truck and go get lunch while this is being resolved?"

"Sure. Jasmine should still have the keys."

When they arrived back at the shelter, the problem was still not resolved. Aubrey took Daniel on a tour of the facility she knew well by now. They took a seat on a bench in the grassy courtyard where they watched people get acquainted with their potential new pets.

Aubrey looked up at the sky. "I need to go talk to Cindy. I don't like the look of the sky to the west."

Once they arrived back at Patton Aviation, Aubrey and Daniel helped unload the four dog crates. Rain came down in torrents, and the wind whipped the windsocks and desert scrubs. The FBO's manager shut the hangar's main door.

"I'm sorry. We're going to have to wait it out. I was hoping to be home for dinner."

Daniel shrugged. "I've been on the scene of plenty of incidents involving people going out in the wrong weather. Better late than never, right?"

Aubrey took a seat beside him on the couch.

After a few hours of talking and playing cards, the storm showed no sign of letting up. Aubrey arranged for them to stay in the pilot's lounge of the FBO overnight, then took two leashes off the top of one crate.

"Ready to get wet?" She handed Daniel a leash.

"With you...always."

She laughed. He took a leash from her, and they took two dogs at a time to a patch of grass to do their business.

Once the dogs were secure and Aubrey and Daniel were soaked, they made their way to the bathrooms to shower off and warm up.

Aubrey changed into the sweatsuit and T-shirt from the overnight bag she always kept in the plane. Her face fell when she came out of the bathroom to see Daniel in his clothing still wet from the rain.

He shrugged. "They'll dry eventually."

The manager appeared in the doorway of the lounge. "I'm leaving. My co-manager will arrive around seven in the morning. Help yourself to what's in the freezer in the breakroom as long as it doesn't have a name on it." He motioned toward a door. "Mostly Hot Pockets. Also, if you go out the side door, it will lock if you let it close, so you won't be able to get back in."

"Good to know." Aubrey smiled at the man in his early 50s. "Thank you again for letting us stay here. Hotels are hard to find with four dogs."

"No problem." The manager nodded and left.

After a couple of games of Jenga, Daniel and Aubrey went to the break room to survey the dinner choices. He heated up a chicken, cheddar, and broccoli pocket for Aubrey and a ham and cheddar for himself. Once again, they settled on the couches in the pilot's lounge.

He watched her for a moment. Her nearly dry hair fell just past her shoulders. If he kept staring, she was going to notice.

As if on cue, she locked eyes with him. "What are you thinking about so hard over there?"

He chuckled under his breath. "Well, I don't know if telling you this is proper etiquette or not, but I'm trying to start an FWB relationship."

She wiped a dot of cheese off her chin. "Good for you!"

He relaxed against the back of the couch. Aubrey was seemingly unfazed by his revelation. Not only unfazed, but a little relieved.

"So, yeah. Hopefully it will go well."

"I hope so too."

The Hot Pocket felt like a lump in his stomach. She was relieved for sure. Did he want her to be relieved?

Daniel was asleep before Aubrey. Without staring, she watched his sleeping face and the rise and fall of his chest with even breathing. A small smile played on her lips, and she shook her head.

He seemed to be coming around to the idea of other partners. She was happy for him as she had indicated. So, what was the twinge she felt? Did it show? Another partner would help her keep the relationship the way she wanted it. Still, Daniel seemed to pull her in. If he keeps pulling her in, will she be able to get out or lose herself in him? All this time, she had been worrying about him developing feelings for her, ignoring the feelings she was developing for him.

Chapter Twenty-Two

Aubrey always loved Vincent's Market Bistro but only went on special occasions. This Saturday afternoon was perfect for a patio table alongside a wooden planter where spring flowers were beginning to bloom.

Franklin had called Aubrey to ask if their March lunch could be a birthday lunch for her and a guest. There was really only one friend she wanted with her: Daniel.

Daniel and Franklin talked easily over their curly endive salads while she looked on enjoying her heirloom tomato soup.

In the distant past, Daniel was not someone her father would have approved of her spending time with. He wanted her to attend an Ivy League school where she could meet and marry a man up to his standards. Not a man who got his hands dirty for a living. She could no longer deny it. Something had truly changed with her father.

Most of the way through lunch, Daniel turned to Franklin. "Thank you for inviting me to Aubrey's birthday celebration. This place is very nice."

Aubrey excused herself from the table.

"I'm pretty sure I have you to thank. I understand you are the reason Aubrey even agreed to meet with me."

Daniel shrugged. "I'm not sure how I did that, but glad to help."

"If I may switch subjects for a moment, you really did well for yourself working for Nate."

"Yes."

"I had gotten to know Nate though Aubrey's flying." He paused for a moment. "The day Aubrey stormed out of Lorraine's and my life, I was up all night worried sick about where she had gone and what might happen to her out there. Of course, she had a plan I knew nothing about. The next morning, Nate called to tell me she would be living in his guest house and working at Skyways while she finished high school. I couldn't have been more relieved. I knew Nate and Justine would look out for her, and they didn't have ulterior motives."

He and Daniel handed off the empty dinner plates.

"Periodically, he would call me or Lorraine. He let us know when she got her pilot's license and her nursing degree. Mostly all he would tell us is that she was okay and happy. Early on, he promised he would call if anything ever happened to her, so for a lot of years, I knew she was alive, but not much else."

Aubrey returned right as the server set the coffee cups and dessert plates on the table.

"Well, at any rate, I hope Aubrey doesn't give you too much of a difficult time."

Aubrey laughed.

"There are a lot of strong women in my circle. I'm used to it."

"And one of them is your daughter, right?"

"Oh yes." Daniel pulled out his phone, showing Franklin his best picture of Makenzie.

Aubrey's day started with a phone call from Daniel. Nate needed all the mechanics for a private jet that came in early in the morning. Daniel didn't want Mackenzie stuck at home during her spring break visit.

After a beautiful flight with mild chop, the plane approached Sedona. Aubrey started pointing out the red rock formations telling Mackenzie their names. The young woman indicated that she could see how Coffeepot Rock and Chimney Rock looked like their namesakes. It took her a few minutes to see how Chicken Point got its name.

Once they landed on the airport's plateau among those rock formations, Aubrey called an Uber to no avail.

She turned to Mackenzie. "Most of the Uber drivers come from Flagstaff. It's a crapshoot whether or not one will be available. After we tie down, I'll try a cab."

Once in the terminal, Aubrey pulled out her phone again.

"By the way, thank you. I would have found something to do today, but this..." She motioned around herself, "is really great."

"I'm glad. Hopefully I can get us into town without having to walk."

Mackenzie shrugged. "Whatever happens, happens. I'll go outside and look at the wind sculptures."

When Mackenzie returned, Aubrey had just finished talking to the owner of the bike rentals. She turned to Makenzie. "Do you ride?" She motioned to the bikes.

She laughed. "You know who my father is, right?"

Aubrey smiled and handed her a helmet and a form. "Fill this out."

Finally, they reached Tlaquepaque, a high-end shopping area in downtown Sedona. After some browsing in the galleries and shops and enjoying the fountains decorated for spring, the two women made their way upstairs to The Chai Spot.

While they sat on majlis decorated in Pakistani prints, Aubrey told Mackenzie the story of the teahouse. Mackenzie seemed enthralled with the story of love that crossed generations of barriers, and the role chai tea had in bringing two families together.

"I'm not much of a romantic, but that is so cool!" Her dark eyes sparkled.

Aubrey continued, "Not only that, but this restaurant also supports schools and women's financial independence in Pakistan."

"Well in that case, I'm going to buy something from the gift shop."

Aubrey took a moment to stretch and enjoy the peace of the patio. A young couple played Jenga at one of the low tables. Further down, some children colored. One child showed her parents the completed picture.

When the female owner set down the tray of tea and pastries, Aubrey introduced her to Mackenzie, and they chatted for a few moments.

"You come here a lot?" Mackenzie asked when the other woman left.

"A few times a year, I'd say."

A gentle breeze fluttered the bright green leaves of the trees that surrounded the patio on two sides.

"It's nice here." Her face turned serious. "I'm glad we came and that we are getting a chance to talk."

"Me too. What's on your mind?" Aubrey smiled.

"My dad. He's a great guy."

Aubrey only nodded.

"He gave up the best years of his life for me instead of shirking his responsibilities like some guys would have done. He quit baseball because he needed to work more along with keeping his grades up and taking care of me. He gave up the college life that I am now loving."

She sipped her tea and appeared to collect her thoughts. "He's enjoying life now, and I'm more than happy for him. But I'm afraid he's going to get hurt."

"You mean by me?"

She picked up a pastry, then set it on her plate without taking a bite. "Yes."

Aubrey took two bites of her pastry while choosing her next words. "Daniel and I have an understanding."

"I think I know about this 'understanding'." She put her fingers in quote signs. "I believe you're a good person, and I'm not judging you. But I also think my dad is talking a good game about all this freedom he claims he wants. He also talks about you...a lot. There are some other women he talks about, and I've now met them. But he doesn't talk about them the way he talks about you."

"Daniel's a big boy. If things change on his part, I'm sure he'll tell me."

Mackenzie turned toward a couple ascending the stairs.

"You're probably right. He would. I'm just protective of him like he is of me."

After biking uphill back to the airport, the two women enjoyed another beautiful flight. When they landed back at Deer Valley, the Skyways crew had just finished up work on the private jet that was now in the southeast run-up area.

Daniel and Mackenzie embraced before Daniel turned to Aubrey. "I think we at least owe you dinner tonight. Plus, I want to hear about the day from both of you."

Aubrey turned to Mackenzie when Daniel focused his attention on leashing Briscoe. Mackenzie nodded.

Daniel and Mackenzie made their way along the Courthouse Butte Loop in Sedona. The trail had some beautiful scenery and great views of the rock formations as Aubrey had said. The wide lane was alive with flowering bushes and insects. It was Mackenzie's last full day in Arizona, and Daniel drove her to Sedona where she wanted to hike one of the trails after seeing the town with Aubrey. Soon, the trail narrowed into a path framed with pinion and juniper pine trees. When they reached the north end of the Courthouse monolith and spied the Rabbit Ears, Mackenzie wanted to stop and take in the view.

"Those boulders over there look like a good place to sit for a moment." Mackenzie motioned toward a formation of about five boulders from where a family had just gotten up after their break.

Daniel filled Briscoe's portable water bowl. He and Mackenzie took a moment to sip from their water bottles and look out at the view in silence.

Finally, Mackenzie turned to Daniel. "I like Aubrey. As you know, I wasn't sure about her at first."

"I know." He smiled at her. "I appreciate you looking out for me. What changed your opinion?"

"Seeing the two of you together and allowing myself to get to know her. You two have fun together, and maybe that's what it's about right now."

He gave her a quick side hug.

"Speaking of fun and friends. How are you doing with your friend group?"

"Enough fun with enough focus on studies."

"Good."

She leaned into him while he put an arm around her. They sat in silence, admiring the Sedona vista.

Chapter Twenty-Three

A spring breeze cooled Daniel's apartment through open windows early on a Sunday evening. He and Sonja cuddled on the couch eating popcorn and watching a movie. She had brought over a comedy that she said he would love. Sonja burst out laughing at certain parts where he could only smile.

When the movie ended, he took Sonja in his arms, kissing her slowly. She melted against him. The feel of her full lips on his and her breasts against his chest caused a powerful surge to course through him.

She slid off the couch. With a fire in her eyes, she reached out for his hand.

Aubrey stood at the tiled countertop and mixed mayonnaise and mustard into the bowl of potatoes and onions while Justine sliced zucchini for the grill.

"How are Ionna and Mykola working out renting your guest house? I'm sure they miss their home in Ukraine, but they're probably glad to be here."

"Yes, on both counts. They keep the place spotless and even help us maintain the yard. This is all while Ionna works a full-time job and Mykola has a full load of classes. She also made the tennis team for her high school."

"Sounds like they both have strong spirits."

"They do. Reminds me of someone else I know." She nudged Aubrey.

"Thank you. But I don't see how it compares. They didn't choose to uproot their lives. It was thrust upon them."

Justine took a bottle of olive oil from the cabinet above her. "I'm not saying what you went through compares to the horrors they probably witnessed."

Aubrey shuddered. "No, definitely not."

Justine brushed the oil onto the zucchini strips. "I'm just saying you didn't ask for the home environment you were raised in, but you built your life in spite of it."

Aubrey rinsed then chopped the fresh herbs from Justine's window box outside the kitchen sink. "I don't know, Justine. Maybe it's having another birthday a few weeks ago, but sometimes I think about changing the way I do relationships."

"Not a damn thing wrong with that. You know I never thought friends with benefits was good for you."

Aubrey mixed the herbs into the potato salad. "I know, but it's comfortable and fun. Committing to one guy feels downright terrifying."

Nate came through the back door to get the platter of zucchini. "Chicken's almost done."

"Great. The potato salad's done except for the eggs," Aubrey said.

Justine looked toward the door Nate had just departed through. "Not everything scary is bad. I've told you how scared I was to love again."

"I know, and every time you two look at each other, I see how great things turned out. But where's the guarantee that it will work out that way for me?"

"Guarantee? You know there isn't one." Justine dug a serving spoon into the potato salad bowl. "But what do you get if you keep sharing your body with men but not your heart?"

Daniel held Sonja's hand as he walked her to her car. "I'm sorry. I really am. You're damned attractive, but it's just not right between us."

When they reached her car, she gave him a gentle kiss on the cheek. "I understand. I'm disappointed, but it's okay."

He pulled her close and held her for a moment.

She took a step back and looked into his eyes. A breeze tousled her dark hair. "You know where I am and how to reach me if things change."

He watched her drive away, then headed back to his apartment. Once inside, he sat heavily on the couch with his head in his hands.

Yes, he could have gone through with it. He had been ready for action. The feel of Sonja's body, the scent of her perfume all brought on thoughts of Aubrey. Sonja's perfume was more flowery than Aubrey's, the whole feel of Sonja was different. But wasn't that the point?

He had considered following through and showing Sonja a great time, but that wouldn't have been fair to her. He would have been with her but not really with her.

Finally, he gently ended the encounter.

Aubrey's father had just finished paying the check at A&J Brewery.

"I have to tell you, Aubrey, you have expanded my restaurant horizons. There is some great food to be had outside of the expensive places I was stuck on."

"Glad you liked your meal." She smiled.

Little by little, she had come to enjoy her lunches with her father and the talks they had in between. She found herself truly looking forward to their April lunch. Their conversations had become more comfortable as the months passed. Now they were talking about a wide variety of subjects, and they both knew something about each other's lives.

They were walking out into the beautiful afternoon toward their cars.

"Aubrey, I wondered if you could come by sometime soon. Since I am downsizing, I've been going through the house little by little. I found some boxes with some of your things. I'd like you to see them and take what you want. If you take them home with you, you could look through them at your leisure, then do what you want with them."

Aubrey pulled her key fob out of her purse. "If you're free, I'll follow you home now."

Aubrey ran her hands up and down her upper arms as she walked into her childhood home. The place with its cherrywood furniture looked mostly the same as when she stormed out on her eighteenth birthday. There were a few decorating changes, a different painting on one wall and some new vases in the family room. She tried to swallow a lump in her throat. This house had been the backdrop of some of her most painful memories, but also some wonderful times in her life.

"The boxes are in your old room," He said, heading down the hall ahead of her toward the master bedroom.

Due to the split floorplan, Aubrey headed in the opposite direction through the family room. She took a deep breath before turning the handle. She caught her breath when she opened the door. The room was made up and cleaned up, but it was also just the same as she had left it. Three boxes of various sizes sat on the multi-hued purple comforter.

None of the boxes were heavy, so she took all three out to her car at once and loaded them into the trunk. When she came back in, she met Franklin entering the living room from the hallway.

"I just finished loading the boxes. Thank you."

"Can I interest you in one of my homemade mudslides?"

Did she want to spend time in this house with him? So much had happened and so much had changed since their last conversation here.

"Sure, just minimal alcohol like you did when I was a teen. I'm driving, after all."

"Coming right up." He smiled.

She took the arcadia door to the back patio and sat on one of the cushioned outdoor chairs, taking in the natural desert landscaping. The furniture set was different from the one they had when she was growing up.

Her father soon joined her, handing her a mug containing a mudslide with extra chocolate syrup.

She took a sip. "I haven't found a place yet that makes mudslides as good as yours." She glanced over at her father who was sitting stiffly in a chair opposite hers. "You okay being out here? Is it too hot?"

She started to rise to help him, but he gently waved her off.

"It's not too hot. I just haven't been out here since the evening I decided to contact you."

She cocked her head. "Why?"

"I didn't tell you everything about that night…Here goes." He shifted in his chair. "I was sitting out here listening to the sounds of nature realizing how alone I really was."

Aubrey's heart quickened.

"I had been feeling more and more dissatisfied with my life and slipping into a depression. That night, I had hit a low point. I finished my drink, took a straight shot of whiskey, and wrote a note which I stuck to the front door for Alejandra to call the police rather than come in."

Hard as she tried to calmly listen, tears stung Aubrey's eyelids and fell.

"I'm sorry," he said and handed her a box of tissues from the table beside him.

"Keep going." She dabbed at her eyes.

"I then went to the safe to get the 9 mm. I was about to pull the trigger when your face came to mind. I decided I couldn't do it without talking to you one last time and telling you that I realized my mistakes in raising you. Of course, you were headstrong and wouldn't contact me just because I wanted you to. This gave me time to rethink my plan. I guess I could say you and your stubbornness saved my life."

Aubrey dabbed at her eyes with her third tissue. "Dad, if you're thinking that way at all, you need to get help."

"Don't worry. I am. I'm seeing a guy who specializes in men like me. Wealthy, powerful, used to having their own way who've realized how much their life sucks. I'm seeing a lot of things through him including how grateful I am that you decided to rebuild something with me."

"Where is the gun now?"

"In the safe. I haven't touched it since that night."

"I want it."

His eyes widened for a second but then he nodded and led her to the safe.

Aubrey called Daniel after leaving her father's house. He was just leaving work, and they agreed to meet at Panda Express near the airport. They chose an outdoor table at the edge of the AMC Theater's courtyard.

She wiped her eyes after relaying the story to him. "I didn't expect any of what he said. He always seemed so.... invincible."

Daniel slowly nodded. "But we both know nobody is."

Aubrey silently watched the theater goers amble through the various movie advertisements in the four-sided marquees.

Daniel brushed the back of her hand with his thumb. "You want to come over?"

She met his eyes. "Yeah. I do."

Aubrey pulled Daniel to her and kissed him hard on the lips as soon as he put his keys on the hallway table.

He gently pushed her back. "Hang on. I figured we would talk more once we got here."

"I don't want to talk anymore."

"Okay."

He looked into her eyes and stroked her face, then tilted his head down to softly kiss her. His lips trailed down her neck into the hollow of her throat before he guided her T-shirt up her torso and over her head. His lips found hers again while he cupped a breast through her soft pink bra.

She backed away only slightly to once again look into his face. The tenderness in his eyes seemed to reach her very core. She was without words.

He reached out a hand to lead her to his bedroom.

Once in his darkening room, he closed the blinds and removed his shirt. She reached out and put his hands to her back. He unhooked her bra, meeting her forehead with his as he slid the garment down her arms. One more lingering kiss before he dropped to his knees and slid off her jeans and panties, then rested his head against her abdomen for a moment. When he stood again, he unfastened his jeans. Aubrey reached into his end table drawer for a condom. From where she now sat, Aubrey slid both his jeans and briefs down his thighs. After sheathing him, she pulled him down onto her. Once he entered her, they found a slow, gentle rhythm. Her eyes took in every detail of his face as the intensity built until the moment nothing existed but his face and the waves of pleasure that gripped and released her.

Daniel lie awake holding Aubrey, taking in the scent of her hair and skin. She fell asleep as soon as they were in the spoon position. Tonight, as they looked into each other's eyes, he could feel himself being pulled deep into her. Every touch, every kiss, every gentle thrust was a point of no return.

He closed his eyes and listened to her even breathing along with the now familiar hum of the ceiling fan. Had he taken it too far tonight? Tonight? Too far was so far away, he would need a damn telescope to see it.

Aubrey awoke and lie awake in the darkness listening to the ceiling fan along with Daniel's rhythmic breathing.

Sex made falling asleep so easy, and last night she went right out. But now at 3:00 she was wide awake. Being with Daniel was different than any other man she had been with in the last several years. That difference had been whispering at the back of her consciousness. Now she could no longer ignore it. She wanted to jump out of bed and run away as far as she could. Yet, she wanted to stay in his bed by his side and never leave.

For a long time, sex had been about fun and experiencing different people. Her friends with benefits arrangements satisfied and protected her. Something had gone very wrong. Tonight, she didn't have sex with Daniel with only her body. Tonight, she had made love with him with her heart. Why was her life unraveling so quickly? Quickly? No, it had been unraveling slowly for months now. It seemed to start around the time she met Daniel.

Aubrey quietly got out of bed; thankful she did not disturb him. After putting on her panties, she padded down the hall, recovering her T-shirt from the glass-topped end table. She shut herself into the hall bath seconds before sobs shook her whole body.

When Daniel's alarm chimed, the sun was visible behind the blinds. Aubrey was not beside him, but the sheets and pillows were slightly warm. He heard movement, and the sound of the refrigerator and cabinets being opened and closed. He put on the pair of lounge pants he had hanging over a chair and pulled a clean T-shirt out of a drawer.

When he came into the kitchen, he saw Aubrey taking a dozen eggs out of the fridge. "Sit down, I'll make breakfast today so you're not late for work."

The sight of her in her T-shirt and panties woke him right up.

Daniel kissed her cheek. "Why don't you sit down, and I'll make you one of my favorite breakfasts. I have time."

"Why don't I help you make it?" She smiled.

Soon, they sat down to cornflake crusted French toast with scrambled eggs and strawberries on the side.

Damn, I like having her here. Last night was so hot, yet so beautiful. Now they were making and eating breakfast together.

"What are you thinking about?" she asked in a tone he couldn't quite read.

He looked across the table. She was smiling, but her eyes said she carried a heavy load.

"Wondering how you're doing after yesterday."

"I think I'm working out a lot of things, but I'm good. Thanks for letting me stay."

Daniel shrugged. "No problem. Anytime."

Time was what she clearly needed.

Chapter Twenty-Four

Daniel hadn't heard from Aubrey since their incredible night together where so much had happened in so little time.

For the past few days, he worked and went straight home, only going out to walk Briscoe. Even then, he took him out when there were fewer people out and about. *I guess I need time too.*

Now his fridge and cupboards were running low. Four days of moping around his apartment was enough.

The grocery store was in the opposite direction from Aubrey's house. She would be arriving home from work soon if she worked a day shift. Everything in him wanted to turn around right now and show up at her house. Check on her. No, the voicemail he left two days ago would have to be enough. She knew he was there for her, so she would reach out if she wanted to.

He continued his course to Walmart. Moving on autopilot, he grabbed what was on his list from each aisle.

"Daniel?"

It took him a second to orient himself. Rochelle stood at the entrance to the bread aisle with a concerned look.

"Oh hey."

"Hi. I just got back into town after taking care of some family business. How have you been?"

"Good."

"You know, I watched you for at least five minutes. You didn't notice you were being observed. That doesn't reflect well on an ex-cop. Is everything alright?"

"Not really. The truth is, I could use an ear."

After he and Rochelle got their groceries to their respective homes and unloaded, Daniel drove her to a nearby Sonic. Over sundaes, Daniel poured out the story of his relationship with Aubrey from beginning to present.

"You've got it bad." Rochelle shook her head. "How long have you known you were in love with her?"

"I think I've known for a while now, but it truly hit me the last night we spent together. After I couldn't follow through with Sonja."

"And you won't declare yourself to Aubrey because you are afraid of losing her?"

He sighed and dropped his forehead into a hand. "Yeah." He looked back at Rochelle. "Wrong reason, right?"

She chuckled. "Wrong reason. If all you wanted was friendship with sex, I'd say keep going. You obviously want more. And you know what? Since you want more, you deserve more."

Carmella called while Aubrey was in the middle of flying back to Deer Valley after going to the Chandler Airport where gas was cheap that day. The clear sunny afternoon lit up the desert below her, causing the hills to cast slight eastward shadows. She was too close to Deer Valley to answer her friend. Time to listen to the ADIS and radio the tower.

Once she landed, she called Carmella who was in the mood for a Mani/Pedi and asked if Aubrey would join her. After a few long, busy days in three ERs, and the recent interpersonal turmoil, a little pampering sounded nice.

The two women met at Carmella's favorite nail salon where they were seated side by side right away. The warm foot bath relaxed her whole body. Nice change of pace.

She turned to Carmella. "So, miss bride-to-be. When are we going dress shopping?"

"Soon. I'm trying to coordinate with my mom and some family members. I'll have a whole entourage helping me pick out the perfect dress."

"Are you going with white, or will you decide once you get there?" Aubrey's foot twitched as the nail tech went a little too light with the pumice sponge.

"Are you kidding? My family will flip if I don't wear white. Never mind that Brock and I have been living together for two years. White is tradition. I know you won't wear white at your wedding."

Aubrey's heart twisted while tears sprang to her eyes.

Carmella turned. "Oh! Aubrey, I didn't mean...It's just that you buck the system on everything. I've always admired you for making your own decisions. I still listen to my family and others too much."

Aubrey leaned her head against the cushioned chair, taking a moment to calm herself. "I don't know that I'm ever getting married."

"That's up to you, but can you really do FWB forever?" Carmella asked. "Why don't you try being exclusive with someone? That Daniel guy, for instance. The way you talk about him, it sounds like he'd be a good choice."

Daniel finished reattaching the cowling of a Beech Baron when Nate locked his office for the day.

"Done?" Nate asked.

"Yeah. I'll walk out with you."

Should he ask, or shouldn't he? Aubrey's lifestyle was none of anyone's business. What Nate knew or didn't know wasn't any of Daniel's business. *What the hell. Here goes.*

"Nate, what do you know about Aubrey's lifestyle?"

"More than she thinks I do. Why?" Nate took a moment to lock the lobby door.

"Well, she and I have been spending time together, and I committed the cardinal sin in her book."

Nate sighed and shook his head. "Oh no. TAV?"

"I'll meet you there."

Daniel sipped his beer while Nate dished up some drunken fries onto an appetizer plate. The loud conversations and 80s heavy metal on the juke box provided a hedge of privacy.

Nate motioned for Daniel to have some fries. "I love that girl. She's the daughter I never had. So many times I've wanted to shake some sense into her. That feeling got stronger when you came to Skyways. She's got so much to offer. Any guy would be lucky to have her, but not just any guy deserves her. With this friends-with-benefits thing, she's wasting her time with men who don't. You? You're the kind of guy I would love to see her with. Aubrey has a friendly, easy manner with nearly everyone, but there's something different when she interacts with you. You seemed to have found a secret entrance. No pun intended."

Daniel looked down at his plate as heat rose to his face. He looked back at Nate after gaining control. "So, you think I should tell her?"

"If you don't, nothing changes. Is that okay with you?" Nate asked. "If you do, you either get a great gal or a broken heart. Is it worth the risk?"

The April weather was a little warm for an early afternoon hike at the conservation park. Daniel's T-shirt and hat were soaked when he and Aubrey reached the amphitheater and sat down on one of the natural, stepped seats.

She took off her hat and poured some water from her bottle over her hair, then replaced her hat.

She turned to Daniel. "Sorry it's been a bit since I called. I've had a lot to think about, and I've been working."

"Understandable. I was fine to give you the space you needed." His stomach clenched. "I've been doing some thinking myself."

"Oh. About what?"

He took a moment to think. She took a drink from her bottle and looked around.

"The last time we were together, it hit me full force that I broke one of your hard and fast rules."

He could see in her face that she was trying to keep control of her expression. Her breathing did an uptick. This could be a good sign. Maybe.

He took a quick swig of water. "I'm in love with you, Aubrey. And I didn't fall in love with you last time we were together. I've been in love with you for a while now."

He thought he saw something flash across her face, but it was gone before he could fully take it in.

"I don't know how you feel about that, but I had to tell you."

A tear slid down her cheek. "Daniel, you don't want me. I'm a mess."

He looked her in the eyes. His heart melted. "I understand that. But it doesn't change how I feel. You're a mess, but you're also everything I've been holding out for."

"There's no way I can be what you want or need."

"Are you telling me I don't know what's right for me?"

"Look, If I'm exclusive with you, then I'm fully exclusive. No more FWBs."

"That's what I want, and I'm hoping you do too."

She stopped and looked down for a long moment. When she looked up again, tears were streaming down her face. "I don't know if I can do that. Damn it, Daniel. I am in love with you, but I'd rather keep things as they are and be with you and my other friends."

His heart was now a rock in his stomach. It was time to say what he didn't want to say. "I can't do that anymore, Aubrey. I want an exclusive relationship, and I want it with you."

"And I'm broken and can't be that for you."

"You're not broken, Aubrey. You don't have to be anything for me. If you love me, that's enough."

"No, it's not because I love you, but I can't change my whole life for you. I'm really not what you want."

He choked back the tears until he couldn't fight them any longer. "Stop telling me I don't know what I want. You clearly know what you want, though."

He stood, but she remained seated, crying freely without words.

Every cell in his body seemed to boil. "You know how to find me if anything changes."

The greens, grays, and browns of the desert were a blur as he stormed to his truck.

"Are you okay? We saw that guy standing over you." A female voice broke through her tears.

Aubrey looked up at a couple in their 50s. She must have looked like hell.

"Yes, I'm fine. He was not a danger to me. Thank you, though."

"Okay. He stormed off. Do you need a ride somewhere?" the man asked.

"No, I drove myself. Again. Thank you."

She rose and headed for the parking lot without looking back. Hopefully Daniel had time to get to his vehicle and would be gone from the parking lot before she got there.

He wanted her. Only her. He wanted her to give up her relations with her friends. He wanted her only for himself. Could she do that? She just told him she couldn't. She suspected he had fallen in love with her. Hearing him say it, though....

Love. Love was dangerous. How long had her mother stayed with her father because she loved him? How many times had her father told her he loved her? Many as long as she was what he wanted her to be.

Then Chad. Chad may have loved his ex-wife but used the word on Aubrey for his purposes. Now Daniel wanted her to be something she may not be able to be. She just needed to get home and take a shower.

Her phone chimed. *Daniel? Visiting Nurses.*

Aubrey quickly grabbed her purse, locked her car, and headed for the elevators. She huffed. Chad was coming toward her. Their eyes met, so avoiding him wasn't possible.

He smiled. "We meet again in a parking garage. This is becoming a habit."

"I'm running late."

"No, you're not. At this hour, you were likely called in last minute, so they're expecting you as soon as you can get there."

She stopped and huffed again. "I've seen Katie a few times recently. Nice rock on her hand."

He nodded. "Look Aubrey, I'm not the arrogant son-of-a-bitch who took advantage of your youth and naivety. When I had the affair with you, I thought I could have whatever I wanted whenever I wanted. I can't, and I'll pay for my indiscretions the rest of my life. I'm going to do it right this time."

"Well, for Katie's sake, I hope so." She stepped around him.

When she reached the pediatric floor, the first face she saw was her friend Andrew.

"Hey Aubrey. Thank you so much for coming. We were already short staffed and then Patrice had to go home."

She smiled brightly, hoping to hide her turmoil. "No problem."

He turned, but she stopped him and lowered her voice. "What are you doing after work?"

"Nothing."

"My place?"

Daniel drove straight home, collected his bat, and headed for the batting cages.

Was it worth the risk, Nate had asked. If you don't tell her, nothing changes, he said. Everything had changed in a matter of moments. Now what? Rochelle said that if he wanted more, he deserved more.

Daniel set up the pitching machine and took his place with the bat at ready. The machine pitched the first ball, and he swung hard. The netting at the far end of the cage rippled. He continued swinging hard at the next several balls, most of them hitting the netting.

Before resetting the machine, Daniel took a long swig of the Liquid IV in his water bottle. He had started drinking it after Aubrey left him the gift bag with various electrolyte mixes. That was so long ago. Nate said Aubrey had so much to offer. She did. But what did that matter now?

He reset the pitching machine and continued swinging hard at every ball.

When Andrew left, the quiet seemed to envelop Aubrey. She turned on Netflix and selected the next episode of her current favorite series, the volume on high.

She couldn't hang with the show, so she shut off the television and slipped out onto her back porch. She curled up on the patio couch and stared into the darkness.

At first, Andrew was turned on by her aggressiveness. But after a short time, he kept trying to slow things down. He gave more input than usual about where and how to touch. She finally realized what she was doing and scaled back. The aggressive, animalistic drive didn't go away, but she held back for the sake of mutuality. Eventually, they were both satisfied. Andrew, as always, was good natured and understanding.

She was now down to two FWB relationships. Andrew was regular enough, but meeting up with Marlon was something that happened here and there. She needed to find at least one, maybe two more. Aubrey shook her head and sighed. More FWBs was the last thing she needed right now. She needed some time alone.

Chapter Twenty-Five

Daniel awoke and wished he could go right back to sleep for about a week. He had returned to Skyways the Monday morning after the hike and gave his work all the focus of a dangerous situation on the Montana highways. Fortunately, Aubrey hadn't shown up at Skyways, helping him put her out of his mind. The evenings were the hardest, but Daniel found things to do to keep from being alone. One night, he hung out with Steve, his single neighbor. On a couple of nights, he called family to catch up. This morning, his aloneness closed in, making it hard to breathe. Everything in him wanted to show up at Aubrey's house. To what end? She had made her decision.

Briscoe jumped up on the bed. He ran his hands along his dog's back and looked into his warm brown eyes.

Briscoe was the only good thing that came out of meeting Aubrey. He had been warned, but he had also seen signs that she was in love with him because she was. Just not enough to commit to him.

He got up and laced his sneakers, then leashed Briscoe.

The slight coolness of the mid-April morning wouldn't last. From what he had heard, soon, even the mornings would be hot. That was fine. Next week, he would be flying to Colorado. Cooler temperatures and time with Mackenzie would feel great.

The stabbing pain in his heart screamed at him to tell Aubrey he wanted her even if that meant sharing her with 10, 50, or even 100 men. He'd take part of her if he couldn't have all of her.

He continued his course around the complex.

Part of her wasn't enough. It was all of her or none of her. If she couldn't give him all, he needed to find someone who could. No more compromising.

"Aubrey...?"

Her half-empty plate came back into focus.

"I...I'm sorry, Dad. What did you say?" The noise and bustle of PF Changs swirled around them.

"I said, I think I found a buyer for my half of the business."

"That's great." It came out flat. Sounding cheerful didn't work anymore.

"Hey. Are you okay?" The lines around his eyes seemed to deepen.

"No. Daniel told me he's in love with me." Tears began to well up, but she maintained control like she had for so many years around her father.

"That's good, right? Or is there something I don't know?"

The server appeared, and Aubrey asked for a box for her honey chicken. Franklin asked for the check to be brought right away.

"You told me after you met him that he's the real deal. You're right. He is." A few tears trickled down her cheeks.

"Okay. Let's go talk in my car."

Her heart began to race. How many one-sided "talks" had they had in his vehicles? Still, she had to get somewhere private and fast.

She quickened her pace and climbed into the passenger side of the Escalade. *What the hell am I doing?*

When the door shut, the dam burst. Her stomach clenched as tears flowed while the rest of the world went about its business in the shopping center's parking lot.

Her father cautiously put a hand on her shoulder and for once just let her cry. No demands to stop immediately. No lectures about how this looks.

"I don't know what's going on, but if there's anything I can do. Anything."

Her tears stopped abruptly. "Anything you can do? I'd say you've done enough."

"I know I have." He lowered his head for a moment.

"Do you know what I do, Dad? I do friends-with-benefits. If you don't know what that is, it means I have sex with men who I consider friends, but there's no commitment. And yes, I did say men and friends, plural. I can't give my heart to a man. The one I did give my heart to years ago, had a beautiful wife and one and a half kids at the time...Now Daniel."

Fresh tears coursed down her face.

He nodded silently handing her a handful of tissues from the center console, his face flashing many emotions at once. He seemed to fight against the urge to say something.

When there were no more tears left and the box of tissues had been depleted, Aubrey took a deep breath and held her father's gaze. "I need a break from our lunches. I just do. I'm sorry."

"I understand." His voice caught. "I'll take you home."

Once in front of her house, she slipped out of the Cadillac. The door shut with a quiet thud behind her.

When Daniel arrived at Skyways, Nate and Justine were in Nate's office looking through some paperwork. No one else was there yet. *Good.* Yesterday was his Sunday to man the FBO, giving him a lot of time to think.

He took a deep breath, put on his Highway Patrol face, and tapped on the plexiglass. Both smiled and motioned him in.

"Morning, Dan. How can we help you?" Nate put the paperwork aside, giving Daniel his full attention.

Justine's smile turned to concern.

Another deep breath, trying to unclench his stomach. "I'll get right to the point. Aubrey and I had a pretty major falling out a couple of weeks ago. I noticed she hasn't been here since. This place is a second home to her, and I can't keep her from it."

Justine's eyes welled up. *Damn it. It's like hurting my mother!*

He turned away from Justine, focusing on Nate. "As hard as this is, I think it would be better all-around if I sought work elsewhere. I'll stay until you find someone, then I need to figure out what to do. I've been happy here in Arizona, but I'm also considering moving back home. I don't know yet."

Nate was silent for a moment. Daniel's heart twisted.

"Well Dan, I'm really sorry to hear that. I mean you're Skyways family now as much as she is. I'd like to think you two can coexist here."

"Not to be disrespectful of her, but I think that may be easier for her than it will be for me."

"Okay." Nate paperclipped the papers he'd been holding. "We'll get things rolling on your resignation when you get back from Colorado."

Aubrey had just finished triaging an eight-year-old girl with a fever and walked her and her parents to the waiting area. "It's pretty slow tonight, so you should be seen shortly."

She then headed toward the break room. Dinner time.

Halfway through her dinner, the head nurse barged into the break-room. "Suicide attempt coming in. Fifteen-year-old girl. Pills."

Aubrey shoved her lunch cooler back into the refrigerator and ran to help set up the room where the teen would be treated.

As if on cue, the moment the room was ready, the ambulance pulled up outside and paramedics unloaded the gurney carrying the unconscious girl. One paramedic helped her sobbing mother down from the vehicle.

The social worker on call approached the mother and guided her toward the private room down the hall from the organized chaos of the treatment room. Aubrey followed the gurney into the room, then helped guide the tube of the stomach pump down the girl's esophagus. She then stepped back, allowing a CNA to clean vomit off the girl's mouth and chest. In a few minutes, Aubrey would help administer the charcoal.

Had the mother found her daughter in time? Would the stomach pump and charcoal save her? Right now, all they could do was wait and find out.

After the teenage girl was treated and admitted, things slowed down. Aubrey decided she would check the stock room and restock any bins that were low.

When the girl named Felicia regained consciousness, it was hard to tell if she was relieved or disappointed that her life had been saved. Maybe both. The teen had recently come out, and her father didn't take it well.

She couldn't keep the memory of herself at sixteen out of her mind.

Aubrey had been sitting in her room after another long lecture about how she had disappointed her father. Again. She was never going to be everything he wanted her to be, and she wasn't going to spend another moment listening to him rant and rave about it. If she were dead, he wouldn't have to worry about what she did and didn't do according to his standards. More importantly, she would never have to hear his bellowing and look into his red face ever again. The question that crossed her mind that day was how to do it.

She was startled out of her morbid thoughts by something hitting the floor. She got up to investigate and found that her Pilot's Logbook had slipped off her school binder. She hugged the logbook to her chest while tears streamed down her face.

No, she had to finish her flight training. Then she had to get her own plane. The turmoil that rolled around inside of her was replaced by more peace than she ever felt in her life. The smallest seed of a plan began to germinate. Her plan for her life.

Of course, the plan had evolved once it was put into action, then continued to do so. Now, where did Daniel fit into that plan? What did she truly want?

Chapter Twenty-Six

Aubrey paid for her salad and sparkling water at the kiosk and found a seat at one of the small tables in the spacious cafeteria.

The last two tumultuous weeks left her wrung out. Two night shifts with a day off to reorient for today's day shift only helped a little. Yesterday, she drove by Skyways and saw Daniel from a distance. His back was to her, and she continued driving to the exit gate. Daniel. What was she going to do about him? Commit or continue? Of course, he had a say in all of this. He may have decided by now that he was better off without her.

After mixing the dressing into her salad, she looked up. Andrew was coming toward her.

The silky black hair she loved running her fingers through had been cut since they were last together.

"Hey Aubrey. I heard you were working in co-care today."

"Yep, I love working with the babies. Have a seat if you're taking a break." She pushed a chair out with her foot.

"Thank you. If I didn't see you today, I was going to call."

His smile did not reach his eyes. Her heart twisted.

"I've been seeing someone for a few months now. We've decided recently to be exclusive."

"Well, that's great. I'm happy for you."

She must have sounded convincing enough because he seemed to relax a little.

"Thank you."

"After all, I'm still your friend, just not with the benefits." She smiled.

The tension returned. "That's just it. She knows I've had a few partners in recent years. She says it would be too awkward to socialize with someone I slept with."

The look in his eyes begged her to understand. "She's perfect for me."

Aubrey smiled. "Then hold on and don't let go. It was great being friends, and it will still be great working with you."

"Thank you." He relaxed again.

When he left the table, he did not look back.

After lunch, Aubrey went about her duties on the maternity floor. Her heart felt like a rock in her chest. Andrew was a friend with benefits. It wasn't like she had ever envisioned a permanent relationship with him. Sure, she would miss their times together. And what was with all the women who were threatened by her? It was her policy that if a man was taken, she wouldn't have sex with him. It was like the fact that she slept with them at all was a problem.

She quietly entered the room of a new mom who was cuddling her two-day old son.

"I'm here to do his assessment. It'll just take me a minute, then you can have him back."

Aubrey smiled as the young woman handed over her precious newborn. When she carried him over to his hospital bassinet, she glanced at his card. The baby's name was Daniel. A new life named Daniel. A new life with Daniel. A wave of clarity washed over her. *I want a new life with Daniel.*

She took a moment to focus on assessing the baby boy. Then seemingly on autopilot she swaddled the infant and handed him back to his mother. "He's doing great."

She hoped the new mom didn't notice that she quickened her pace as she left the room. How long until the end of her shift?

Aubrey finished her paperwork and raced to her Challenger, heart pounding. The day's events had cemented for her what she really had known for months now. She was in love with Daniel and wanted to be with him. Her FWB relationships had served their purpose, but now they no longer satisfied. She wanted Daniel. Not because the sex was so great, but because of who he was and the things they shared. As Marlon had said, the things that were uniquely them.

All the way down the freeway, Aubrey rehearsed what she might say when Daniel answered the door. How should she respond if he rejected her tonight? Argue? Deal? Accept? Of course, accept was the only real option. Tears stung at the thought.

The gate to Daniel's apartment complex came into view. She calmed herself as she punched in the code and drove by the familiar colors, paths, and lawns toward guest parking. One deep breath, and she rang the doorbell.

She heard Briscoe's yipping, and her heart quickened at the click of the door unlocking from the inside.

Sasha appeared in the doorway. "Aubrey, I only answered because I saw it was you."

Aubrey crouched down and ran her hand over Briscoe's silky fur. "Where's Daniel?"

"In Colorado helping Mackenzie secure housing for next year."

"That's right. I forgot he was going out of town. Damn. I really need to talk to him in person."

"He'll be back Monday evening."

"That will have to do." She smiled, scooping up Briscoe and handing him to Sasha. The little dog licked Sasha's nose.

Once she was back in her car, everything in her wanted to dial Daniel's number. No, he was with Mackenzie, and this conversation needed to be had in person.

Daniel approached baggage claim. Mackenzie was already there waiting for him. Her beaming face was salve to his wounded heart. His fellow passengers swarmed around them greeting family, friends, and business contacts.

After he pulled Mackenzie into a hug, she stepped back. "You look like hell."

"It's nice to see you too."

"No, seriously, you look like you need to talk."

"I'm fine, Mac. Let's go to your dorm and meet your friends."

She studied his face. *Damn it. Does she have to do that?* He looked toward the ground.

"Your cop face doesn't work with me. My friends can wait until tomorrow."

"Okay. The last few weeks have been hell." Daniel grabbed his bag off the carrousel.

"Come on. I know a good place in town."

Aubrey pulled up in front of Marlon's hangar. Another pilot, James, was laughing with him at the card table in the corner.

"Hey Aubrey," they said in unison when she approached.

"Grab a beer or soda if you're staying." Marlon motioned to his fridge.

Aubrey opened his fridge and pulled out an orange Poppi soda. At that moment, James looked at his watch. "As usual, time flies." He laughed at his own pun with pearl teeth against ebony skin. "I gotta go." He stood and smiled at Aubrey making a tipping-hat motion.

"See you later." Marlon waved.

"Yeah. Unless I see you first."

Once James drove off, Aubrey sat in the chair he had occupied. A hot breeze blew into the hangar.

"Well. Nice to see you on a Saturday morning, Aubrey. What brings you over?"

"Needed to drop some stuff off at my hangar. Also, we need to talk."

He tilted his head. His smile drooped a little. "It looks to me like things are about to change between us."

Aubrey nodded. "I've fallen in love, and if he'll have me, I will be in an exclusive relationship. If he won't, I've decided to take some time alone, then maybe find someone to be exclusive with."

"Well, that's wonderful. You deserve to be with someone who will love you. We both know that what we had was not about love."

Aubrey teared up and nodded. "No, but it was great."

He squeezed her hand. "For that, I'm glad."

She rose and headed to her car.

"Aubrey."

She turned toward him.

"If he turns you down, he's crazy."

Her heart lightened. Daniel wasn't crazy.

Chapter Twenty-Seven

Aubrey put two frozen waffles in the toaster. She had alerted Visiting Nurses that she would be unavailable today. Daniel's plane would land at Sky Harbor at 4:35 p.m. and she would be there at Baggage Claim waiting for him.

His arrival was hours away. She was not going to sit around all day watching the clock. She ran her finger along a shelf in her breakfast nook, leaving a line in the dust. There was a similar layer of dust on the coffee tables, end tables, and other shelves. The floors needed to be vacuumed too. She had been so busy and emotional the last few weeks that her routine maintenance had fallen by the wayside.

Giving the house a good cleaning was the perfect way to pass the hours until she could get ready to meet Daniel. Hopefully, he would cancel his Uber and leave the airport with her. Unless he decided he was done with her. Her heart sank. She may have to watch him get into an Uber and ride away.

The phone rang right as she turned on her dishwasher.

Aubrey took off from runway 7 Left then banked her plane to the northeast. The desert turned to trees as she headed toward Show Low on the Arizona side of the New Mexico border. The most recent wildfire in New Mexico was advancing so quickly that residents had to be evacuated. Several shelters and makeshift shelters near Show Low stepped up to house the dogs and cats and other pets.

She loved flying any time of the year, even the warmer months with more turbulence. Smooth or turbulent, the mild swish of the back end of the V tail was as comforting and familiar as a rocking chair.

There would only be enough time for two trips before flying home and heading straight for Sky Harbor. She could help out more tomorrow if need be.

Instead of being freshly showered and made up to meet Daniel, she would have to show up as is, smelling of smoke and animals. Oh well. If he truly loves her, he won't care.

The weekend was a success. Next year, Mackenzie would live a short drive from campus with three other girls from her established friend group. Now he took Mac to lunch at a sports bar before she would drive him to the airport for his return flight. A spring breeze made it an ideal day for a patio table.

Daniel tilted the table's umbrella, blocking the direct sun. "I feel good about your living arrangement."

"Me too. Thank you for all of your help."

"You seem sure that the four of you are a good fit."

"We are." Mackenzie dipped an onion ring in ketchup.

"Good, because this is a commitment for a full school year. If anything goes wrong..."

She held his gaze. "You know, you don't have to stay in Phoenix or if you do, there are other airports. Hell, there are airports back home and all over the country that would hire you."

"I've thought about all of that. I really like where I work, but I told Nate I was leaving. If I see Aubrey around before I leave, I'll just have to suck it up. I'll get through this."

She looked him directly in the eye. "Yes, you will. Listen, don't let her hurt you again."

Daniel settled into an open seat next to a woman and a boy who looked to be between seven and nine years old. Other than a brief acknowledgment, neither one engaged Daniel in any kind of small talk. This was a welcome relief as his mood dropped as soon as he boarded the plane.

Going back to Phoenix and back to Skyways. He loved working at Skyways. Nate, Justine, and the team of A and Ps were the best he could have asked for. The whole place brightened even more when Aubrey showed up. Nothing had been started with his resignation. He could tell Nate he changed his mind.

He'd been through relationships ending before. Sometimes he ended it. Other times, the girlfriend ended it. Of course, there were the relationships that ended by mutual agreement. It wasn't fun, but he always got through it. He would get through this as well.

Why did this break up seem so different? Or was it just that she was the most recent? No, it was different. He had fallen for Aubrey like he hadn't since Jen back in high school. He loved her and she loved him. She had told him as much. She loved him but didn't want to give up the fun of her FWB lifestyle. What was he supposed to do with that? Was he supposed to club her over the head, throw her over his shoulder, and take her to his apartment dragging his knuckles the whole way? He would just have to accept the situation and deal with the pain of seeing Aubrey until it alleviated.

The nights in a hotel bed, late-night talks with Mackenzie, and a busy apartment-hunting schedule caught up with him. He fashioned his jacket into a neck pillow, leaned back, and was instantly asleep.

After dropping off the first group of dogs and cats, Aubrey went through the hot start up procedure and took off again to pick up more displaced pets.

When she reached the halfway point, she flipped the fuel selector valve, switching to the left tank. The plane started to shake and began to lose power rapidly.

"What the hell?!" She switched back to the right tank. The engine continued running rough. She pushed the fuel mixture control to full rich.

Aubrey then hit the "Nearest" button on her GPS. The nearest airports were Show Low Regional halfway behind her or Socorro Municipal halfway in front of her.

She pressed the talk button. "Albuquerque Center. 6282 Romeo. My engine just started running rough. It's slightly better at full rich."

She turned on the boost pump. "The boost pump is causing it to run a little better, but it's still shaking a lot."

Aubrey took deep breaths to keep focused. She then started trying different power settings and fuel mixture combinations to get the engine to smooth out.

"I've got it running more smoothly but at low power. Every time I try to go to full power, it starts running rough again."

She set her trim wheel to the best glide speed of 90 mph.

"Roger. Fuel remaining? How many souls are on board?"

"Four hours and just myself. Partial power. Losing altitude at 500 feet a minute."

Beads of sweat formed on her forehead.

When she pulled the prop control to coarse pitch, the plane continued losing altitude but at 200 feet per minute.

She exhaled, relaxing slightly. Her chances of making the airport were better now.

Aubrey visually scanned the immediate terrain and searched for a place to land if she couldn't make the airport. Trees, trees, and more trees. *This is not good.*

She glanced at the GPS to see how far the nearest airport was now.

The plane was running rougher by the minute. She spotted a clearing closer than the airport.

"Albuquerque Center. 6282 Romeo. I'm 50 miles from Socorro and 1,000 feet above the ground. I see a clearing among the trees. I'm going to try to make it there."

"Roger. We will alert the Socorro County authorities."

Tears stung. "Thank you." Her voice caught. "Please alert Skyways Aviation at Deer Valley Airport."

"Roger that."

Aubrey always knew her love of flying might one day lead to her end. *Not today.*

She kept her speed up in any way she could as the plane skimmed the trees much closer than she was comfortable with. She left the landing gear up to avoid flipping over and causing serious injury and damage.

Gas, undercarriage, mixture, prop, seatbelt.

Once above the clearing, she put the plane sideways into a slip to bleed off energy and lower the plane to the ground. The plane descended as gradually as possible under the circumstances. She opened the door to enable her to exit and shut the fuel off to avoid fire. The belly touched the ground, sliding and bumping over the terrain.

She did her best to maintain directional control through the crash sequence. The trees came toward her at an alarming rate. The clearing was ending!

Bam! The Bonanza stopped abruptly and went sideways as one wing caught on one tree followed by the other wing hitting another tree.

The Southwest Airlines 737 touched down smoothly at Sky Harbor. Daniel's flight from Colorado Springs was short, but he still felt cramped and couldn't wait to stretch his legs. Once the fasten seatbelt light went off, he joined several others in standing up and opening the overhead compartments. He first retrieved the bag for the mom and boy who sat beside him. He then took out his carry-on.

Once he exited the plane, he realized that he hadn't taken his phone off airplane mode. He shifted the bag to his left hand then took his phone out of his pocket, getting it back online.

Immediately a text signal chimed. Nate.

There's been an emergency. Ray will meet you at baggage claim and bring you to Deer Valley.

Daniel took off at a run toward Baggage Claim, his heart pounding faster than it normally would at the speed he was running.

Was it Mackenzie or someone back home?

The grave look on Ray's face did nothing to alleviate the anxiety.

"Ray. What the hell's going on?"

Ray looked around, then led him to a less congested area away from the baggage carousel. "Aubrey's plane went down just inside the New Mexico border."

Daniel felt his knees start to give out, and he braced his hand against the wall for support. "Is she....?"

"We don't know anything yet. Franklin chartered a flight to Albuquerque. They're holding the plane for you."

Daniel saw his bag out of the corner of his eye. He ran over and yanked it off the carousel and headed for the elevator, heart pounding and stomach clenched.

Once parked in front of Cutter Aviation, Daniel reached for the door handle, but Ray stopped him.

"Before going to Albuquerque, you need to understand something. Nate and Justine know the area where she went down and they're very upset. Nate says her chances of surviving a forced landing there are not high. You have to be ready for that."

Daniel nodded, then ran into the lobby where Lorraine, Charlie, and Franklin waited. Lorraine picked up her purse and jacket as soon as she saw him.

Daniel locked eyes with Franklin. "Thank you."

Franklin only nodded as they walked through the lobby's back entrance toward the waiting King Air.

Aubrey had moved her emergency duffle bag and overnight bag to the back seat as she knew she would need room in the baggage compartment for kennels. She grabbed the bags then pushed the door open.

After descending the wing, she set the bags down, took a deep breath, and walked around the front of 6282 Romeo to survey the damage. Her heart twisted at the sight of her beloved Romeo with a crumpled engine compartment and leading edges.

She rested her forehead against the sheet metal and began to shake with racking sobs.

Aubrey had no idea how long she stood there like that, but the shadows were longer, and the sun was making its way in the hazy sky toward the western horizon.

Weak and spent, she went back to her emergency bag and took stock. Six bottles of water, four protein bars. That should get her by until search and rescue could get to her. Snow overalls, ski jacket, thermal blanket. Those will come in handy as the temperature in the wooded area was already dropping. Water purifying straw and matches in a water-proof canister. Those wouldn't be needed this time.

Albuquerque Center knew where she went down due to Flight Following. She opened the cargo door. The small flashing light indicating her Emergency Locator Transmitter (ELT) went off as well. Most of the fire department and forest service would be tied up with the wildfires. Even without wildfires, she was in a remote area and knew it could take several hours to get to her. The plane did not catch fire, so in the worst-case scenario, she would sleep in her plane tonight.

Images of Daniel played through her mind like a slideshow. His plane would have already landed. She knew Nate would have alerted her parents to the situation. He would have alerted Daniel too, wouldn't he? He wouldn't be back at Skyways until tomorrow morning. Either way, she was going to get through this and talk to Daniel. For now, she would have to wait.

When the King Air landed in Albuquerque, the small group was met by the airport's manager.

"The New Mexico State Police used data from Ms. Cassen's Flight Following and ELT. According to GPS, she landed the plane in a clearing, so her chances are good."

Lorraine burst into tears and fell against her new husband.

"The State Police are prepping as we speak to helicopter her out. She will be taken to the University of New Mexico Hospital. We will transport you all, so you'll be there when she arrives."

"I need to talk to the captain," Daniel said.

Daniel used his status as ex Highway Patrol to secure a place on the helicopter. They needed all the extra help they could get.

His pounding heart seemed louder in his ears than the helicopter's engine. Looking out over the expanse of trees and mountainous terrain, he knew what Nate meant by her chances of survival being low. But the airport manager said they found her plane in a clearing. Nate had said on a few occasions that she's one hell of a pilot. The grassy clearing was straight ahead. His heart dropped into his stomach at the sight of the crumpled airplane up against the trees at the edge of the clearing.

The helicopter began descending.

Maybe this was a mistake. Maybe he wasn't up to seeing what he was about to see. Just then, movement caught his eye.

Relief washed over him as he and the team cheered.

When the helicopter touched down, he ducked under the rotor blades and ran to her.

Aubrey waved when she saw the helicopter. She shielded her face from the wind created by the blades. When she cautiously looked out, she noticed the first man off the helicopter ran toward her.

"Aubrey!"

She barely heard her name above the engine and rotor blades. As soon as he was past the blades, he removed his helmet and goggles.

"Daniel!"

She ran to him. Tears streamed down her face as he pulled her into his arms. He leaned down to meet his lips with hers. She tasted the salt from his tears as she kissed him gently at first, then harder as he again pulled her to him.

After an emotional reunion at the ER, Aubrey followed the triage nurse to an exam room.

The exam indicated Aubrey would be bruised and sore for a few days, but she was not seriously injured. Franklin had his secretary book rooms at a nearby hotel.

Once settled in their room, Aubrey and Daniel each showered and changed into fresh clothes from their luggage.

"Glad I overpacked this time." He smiled, pulling on a black and gold UC Colorado Springs T-shirt.

Aubrey smiled, looking him over, taking in his features as if for the first time. "Let's go for a walk. I'm still wound up."

Hand in hand, they walked the sidewalks of the hotel grounds.

Aubrey broke the silence. "This day has my head spinning. I've only seen my dad cry once when his mother passed away. And I've never known Nate to cry like he did on the phone."

"We all could have lost you today." Daniel's voice caught.

When they reached an unlit fire pit in the middle of the courtyard, she stopped and took both of his hands in hers. Tears streamed freely down her face. "I was planning to pick you up from the airport today and tell you that I realized how much I love you and want to be with you. I broke off my last FWB relationship while you were in Colorado."

Realization washed over his face.

She wiped her tears on her shirt. "Of course, I needed to find out if you'd still have me. And when you showed up at the crash site today..."

More tears.

He took her face in his hands and kissed her gently, then pulled her close and just held her.

"I want to do this right this time." Daniel dropped to one knee.

Her heart felt like it would burst.

He held her gaze. "Aubrey Cassen, will you marry me?"

Still more tears coursed down her cheeks and onto her shirt. "Yes, I will!"

He arose and pulled her into his arms.

Chapter Twenty-Eight

Aubrey and her mother sat side by side in front of Aubrey's computer scrolling through countless non-traditional wedding dresses.

Aubrey's phone chimed. *You knew this was coming.*

"Excuse me for a minute, Mom." She got up from her office chair and headed to the back patio.

She took a deep breath. *Let her have her say then choose your response.*

"Hi, Mackenzie. I'm glad you called."

"Yes, I waited a few days so as not to shoot from the hip. First, I'm glad you're okay. That had to be scary as hell."

"It was. Scariest thing I've ever been through."

A warm breeze ruffled her hair and carried over the scent of a neighbor grilling meat.

"I'm sure Dad told you I'm not exactly thrilled about you two getting engaged."

"He didn't give me any details, he just said your reaction could have been better, but it could have been worse."

"Sounds like him. Look. I have a dad and a stepdad. Two very different men. As a result, I got the benefit of both of their strengths growing up. I had always hoped that my dad would remarry, and I would get that same benefit. When I met you, I had my concerns, but you were also what I wanted for him. Then I saw him at the airport a few weeks ago...." Her voice caught. "He tried to hide it, but I could see how hurt he really was."

"Mackenzie I -"

"Listen. I'm past the age where you'll be helping raise me. Love me. Hate me. There's not a damn thing you can do to hurt me...Except hurt my dad again. Are you going to get cold feet before the wedding and call it off or decide in a year or two that you miss your old life?"

"No. I am a hundred percent committed to Daniel and the life we are going to build together. If anyone leaves, it's going to have to be him because I'm not going anywhere."

Mackenize was now crying freely on the phone. She took a jagged breath. "That's what I needed to know."

Aubrey rushed into Nate's office where Daniel was already seated. He took her hand in his.

Once her beloved V-tail was recovered, it was taken by trailer to Skyways where the whole crew swarmed to pull the engine and send it off to be rebuilt. While they waited for the results, the Skyways A and P team set out to repair the airframe damage.

Nate folded his hands in front of him. "Okay. The new engine has new spark plugs, wires, and a starter. However, it was still running rough at high power. So, it has to be the fuel system."

"Nate and I have been going crazy looking over the entire system. No debris or contaminates in the fuel. The fuel lines and fuel pump are working fine, " Daniel said.

Nate chimed in, "Then I remembered an incident at the airport several years ago. A guy landed at low power. Turns out, the fuel selector valve was sucking air."

"Is that what it was? It wasn't pilot error?" Aubrey asked.

"No, it was nothing you did and nothing we failed to do," Nate said.

Daniel planted a kiss on top of her head.

Nate slid the keys to the plane across the desk. "We replaced the selector valve, now your plane runs beautifully."

Aubrey's grabbed the keys, pressing them to her chest while tears streamed down her cheeks.

Nate pushed back from his desk. "Let's take it around the pattern."

Fergus Chapel on the field at Wittman Regional Airport was a peaceful oasis amid the buzz and activity of EAA Airventure.

The stained-glass windows depicting various airplanes in flight were vibrant on such a beautiful sunny day.

Aubrey stood just inside the dressing room door with Carmella and Mackenzie. Each held a simple bouquet of three white roses surrounded by a little greenery. After two taps on the door, the wedding coordinator stepped into the room.

"It's time." She beamed at them.

Aubrey smiled back. This was happening. It was really happening.

When Mackenzie exited the room and turned down the small aisle, Aubrey peeked out. Daniel was radiant when he saw his daughter in her flowing, green asymmetrical dress. She spontaneously kissed his cheek when she reached the front. He hugged her and returned her kiss before she took her place.

Carmella squeezed Aubrey's hand, smiled brightly, then proceeded down the aisle in her green dress. Same color as Mackenzie's, but in a style that complemented her very different figure.

Aubrey straightened her sky-blue maxi dress to make sure she wouldn't catch it on her matching low-heeled sandals.

Nothing was going to keep her from Daniel. Not even the billions of butterflies fluttering in her stomach and chest.

She stepped out of the dressing room and took her place at the back of the aisle. Everyone turned to look at her.

Her butterflies disappeared at the sight of Daniel's beaming face.

She made her way up the aisle toward the stone fireplace. Loraine and Charlie stood beside Franklin while Nate and Justine stood behind them in the second row. Across the aisle, Daniel's mother and father along with his sister, brother-in-law, and sister-in-law occupied the front row. A few of Daniel's aunts, uncles, and a cousin stood behind them. Daniel's brother and his best friend Mason who had been the best man at his first wedding stood to his left. The officiant was an airport chaplain.

Aubrey took her place next to Carmella and Mackenzie and turned to face Daniel. His sky-blue shirt and tan Dockers set off his amber eyes which sparkled as they looked into Aubrey's.

Saying her vows of commitment came easy. Aubrey had already given Daniel her full heart. Today just made it official under the law and in the presence of those who loved them.

"You may kiss the bride," the chaplain said with a smile.

When Daniel's lips met hers a current surged from her lips to her core. She pulled him close for another kiss before they headed up the aisle.

The small group went outside onto the lush green lawn. A few Canada geese swam gracefully on the lake. Deli trays adorned the buffet table where people made sandwiches, then gathered at the round tables. Aubrey's heart swelled at seeing her friends and family mingle with Daniel's. She leaned against him. It was only the beginning of their new life together. The party wasn't even over yet. They still had the cake to cut and two champagne toasts to listen to. Who knew what Carmella and Mason would say. Soon after, a tram would take everyone to the flightline for an incredible air show. But for now, Aubrey basked in the warmth of connection. Family united by more than just blood, friendships forged by time and trust, and the love of a true partner. No one knew what challenges lay ahead, but she knew she would never again face them alone.

Acknowledgements

Writing *Flight Plan* was made possible by the wonderful people in my corner. My heartfelt thanks go to my husband David, a general aviation pilot, and my son Michael, an aircraft mechanic (A and P). Your shared aviation expertise helped me create scenes that are authentic and alive.

To my dedicated beta readers – Jen Rice, Polly Gan, Jenny Carry, Teri Hunt, and Becky Ramsdell – Your insights made this novel everything it could be. My critique partners, Carolyn Stephens and Charlotte Whitney, opened my eyes to the subtle layers my story needed, and I am deeply grateful.

A special thank you to Jenny Carry and Ruth Douthitt for the guidance and industry advice you so generously shared, always ready to answer questions big and small. To my editor, Borbala Branch thank you for guiding me through the final drafts with care and precision.

Alongside these incredible people, I am blessed with friends who cheered me on at every turn. Brenda Cummings, Emily Allen, Catherine Reiker, Caitlin Rook, Lisa Carpenter, Katie Metza, Davena Ballard, Christine Corbridge, Terrie Calderon, Teri Lander, and Kristin Costa – your encouragement means more than you know.

Thank you also to my West Valley Chicks book club and the Scottsdale Society of Women Writers. The knowledge and camaraderie shared with you all has been invaluable.

Finally, my deepest gratitude goes to my parents, Mike and Linda Thiel, for their unwavering support of all my endeavors.

About the author

Lynn Campbell is an elementary teacher based in Phoenix Arizona where she lives with her husband and son. As an aviation wife, Lynn has spent countless hours at general-aviation airports in and around Arizona immersing herself in the world of flight. When she isn't writing, teaching, and traveling, she loves exploring new foods, diving into Rock n Roll history, and getting lost in a good book.

Also by

In addition to Flight Plan, Lynn wrote and published suspense thriller Revenge Game in 2022

*In this game, the
prize is her life.*